Englisch

On

Purpose

BOOKS BY J.E.B. SPREDEMANN

(*J. Spredemann)

AMISH GIRLS SERIES

Joanna's Struggle

Danika's Journey

Chloe's Revelation

Susanna's Surprise

Annie's Decision

Abigail's Triumph

Brooke's Quest

Leah's Legacy

SHORT NOVELS/NOVELLAS*

*Amish by Accident**

An Unforgivable Secret - Amish Secrets 1*

A Secret Encounter - Amish Secrets 2*

A Secret of the Heart - Amish Secrets 3*

An Undeniable Secret - Amish Secrets 4*

*Learning to Love – Saul's Story** (Sequel to Chloe's Revelation – adult novella)

A Christmas of Mercy – Amish Girls Holiday

Englisch on Purpose (Prequel to *Amish by Accident*)*

Christmas in Paradise – (Final book in *Amish by Accident* trilogy)

*Love Impossible – Amish Dreams**

NOVELETTES*

Cindy's Story – An Amish Fairly Tale Novelette 1*

Rosabelle's Story – An Amish Fairly Tale Novelette 2*

COMING 2016! (Lord Willing)

A Secret Sacrifice - Amish Secrets 5

Englisch on Purpose

(Prequel to ***Amish by Accident***)

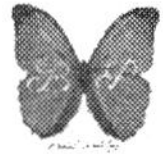

All incidents and characters in this book are completely fictional and derived by the author's imagination. Any resemblance to actual incidents and persons living or dead are purely coincidental.

All Scripture quotations are taken from the *King James Version* of the *Holy Bible*, are not subject to copyright laws in the U.S., and may be freely copied and/or quoted.

Cover design by *iCreate Designs*©

Published in Indiana by *Blessed Publishing*.
www.jebspredemann.com

ISBN: 978-1-940492-13-1
10 9 8 7 6 5 4 3 2 1

Unofficial Glossary of Pennsylvania Dutch Words

Ach – Oh

Ausbund – German hymn book

Boppli / Bopplin – Baby / Babies

Dat / Daed – Dad

Denki / Danke – Thanks

Der Herr – The Lord

Dochder(n) – Daughter(s)

Englischer – A non-Amish person

Fraa – Woman, Wife

Gott – God

Gut – Good

Jah – Yes

Kinner – Children

Maed / Maedel – Girls / Girl

Mamm – Mom

Nee – No

Schatzi – Honey, Sweetheart

Vatter – Father

Author's Note

It should be noted that the Amish/Mennonite people and their communities differ one from another. There are, in fact, no two Amish communities exactly alike. It is this premise on which this book is written. We have taken cautious steps to assure the authenticity of Amish practices and customs. Old Order Amish and New Order Amish may be portrayed in this work of fiction and may differ from some communities.

We, as *Englischers*, can learn a lot from the Plain People and their simple way of life. Their hard work, close-knit family life, and concern for others are to be applauded. As the Lord wills, may this special culture continue to be respected and remain so for many centuries to come, and may the light of God's salvation reach their hearts.

To **Samuel and Polly**…

who remain *Englisch on Purpose* for all the right reasons…May our gracious God continue to bless your wonderful family

CHAPTER ONE

Matthew listened closely. Did he hear something? He peeked over at Maryanna in the darkness, who lay by his side, softly snoring.

A soft click told him all he needed to know. He hastily rose from the bed and pulled his suspendered pants on quietly. He nearly tumbled over his work boots as he tiptoed toward the living room. He flipped the lights on.

"Dad?" His daughter's surprised expression was wrought with anguish.

His muscled forearms crossed his chest. "What are you doing out at this hour? Your curfew was an hour ago, young lady." He pointed to the clock on the wall.

"I…I…uh, Johnny and Judah wanted to stay out longer. I told them I had to be home."

"That's not good enough. Try again." He raised a brow.

"What's going on?" Matthew turned at Maryanna's voice.

"Our daughter is *just now* returning home."

"Matthew, can't we discuss this in the morning? I'm sure Mattie's tired."

Matthew didn't miss the 'thanks, Mom' look Mattie tossed Maryanna. "I think it needs to be discussed now," he insisted.

"Why?" Maryanna challenged him.

"Why? Because this is important, that's why. And by the time she awakens in the morning, I'll have been working a couple of hours. At least."

Their daughter, Rebekah, walked into the kitchen, yawning. "What's going on, Mom?"

"Your sister, here, is late. Once again." Matthew frowned. "You may go back to bed, Rebekah."

Mattie's hands flew up. "I don't know what you want me to say, Dad. I've told you the truth." She yawned. "I'm tired. Can I go to bed now?"

"No." He held out his hand. "Give me your keys."

"But, Dad–"

"Now." Matthew tempered his frustration as best as he could.

Tears welled in his daughter's eyes and she yanked her car keys from her purse.

Matthew clenched his fingers around them. "You're grounded for two weeks."

"But how will I get to school and work without my car?"

"Perhaps you should have thought about that *before* you decided to return home late."

"Matthew, isn't this a little harsh?" Maryanna's hand caressed his back.

Matthew frowned. "No, this is not harsh. We've been over this before. She's had fair warning. She needs to realize there are consequences for her actions." He turned back to their daughter. "Go to bed, Mattie."

"You're just like *Dawdi* Sabastian!"

He grimaced as his daughter flew up the stairs in tears. Being compared to his ultra-strict Amish father was not a compliment by any stretch of the word.

"Are you sure that was the best thing to do?"

Matthew stared at his wife in disbelief. "Listen, Maryanna. I need you to support me. We need to be in agreement."

"I just don't think that was the best thing to do."

"And what would *you* have done?"

"I probably would have waited until tomorrow, then I would have reasoned with her."

"We've tried that already, remember?" Matthew sighed. "Maryanna, do you think it's easy for me to put restrictions on our children? Well, it's not. She knows better. And Mattie staying out late is asking for trouble. Especially if she's with Jonathan's boys."

Maryanna exhaled. "You have a point."

"Okay, Lis, I've had it! My parents are driving me crazy," Mattie ranted. "If they keep this up, I think I'm going to scream."

Elisabeth eyed her best friend. "I can't believe they took your car away."

"Not the car, just the keys. Which is essentially the same thing, I guess." Mattie paced from Elisabeth's bedroom window to her desk, then plopped down in her chair. "I'm thinking of leaving."

"Mattie, don't leave. What am I going to do if you're gone?"

"Come with me then."

"I don't know. It's kind of scary." Elisabeth shook her head. "Where will you go? Who will you stay with?"

"I'm sure I'll find a place. I've been saving up money from my job." Mattie tapped her chin. "I think I'll look up 'Help Wanted' ads in New York."

Elisabeth's eyes widened. "New York?"

"I've always wanted to go there. Why not?"

"But it's so big. And there are *ferhoodled* people there."

Mattie smiled at her Amish best friend. "There are *ferhoodled* people everywhere, Lis. Just look at my cousins." She laughed, thinking of Johnny and Judah and all the mischief the twins had gotten into over the years.

"I can't believe they still have their motorcycles. You'd think Bishop Hostettler would have made them sell them."

"Oh, I'm sure he will when they finally join the church."

"Do you think they will? Because I can see them becoming *Englisch*."

"They said they plan to join the church. I just don't think they're ready to settle down just yet."

"Jonathan," Matthew began, after taking a sip of his root beer.

Jonathan raised his hands in protest, a definitive smirk on his face. "I already know what you're going to say. My boys, right?"

"You've got to give them some restrictions. They've been getting Mattie into trouble. She was late again."

Jonathan's brow shot up. "That's it?"

"It's a big deal when my daughter disobeys me."

"Maybe you should lift her curfew."

"Lift her curfew?" Matthew shook his head. "She's got work and school. She needs sleep at night."

"She's an adult, Matt. She needs to figure out for herself what's important and what's not. Her work and school might suffer a bit, but she could learn a valuable lesson. You and Maryanna won't always be there to tell her what time to be home. She needs to learn responsibility. That could be the best way."

"I don't know…"

"What's the worst-case scenario? She misses a class or loses her job, right?"

Matthew shook his head. "Or she falls asleep driving and kills herself or someone else."

"Our time is in *Der Herr's* hands; you know that."

"I know, I know. But shouldn't I do *something*?"

Jonathan nodded. "Yes. Pray for her. Then leave her in God's hands."

"That's so hard to do."

"Our *kinner* do not belong to us; they belong to *Der Herr*."

Matthew attempted to tamper his frustration. "I realize that, but I still feel that I should be a parent to her."

"There's another option."

"What's that?"

Jonathan rubbed his beard. "You could give her an ultimatum."

Matthew frowned. "A what?"

"Give her a choice: follow the rules of the house or move out."

"That's a tough one. Maryanna'd kill me if I told Mattie that. Besides, where would she stay?"

"She'd figure it out pretty quickly."

Matthew chuckled. "She'd probably move in with you."

Jonathan shrugged. "Her cousins wouldn't mind."

"That would be like a reward for her, I think." He shook his head.

Maryanna stepped into the shop. "Ooh, rewards? I like rewards." She eyed both men. "What are you two up to?"

"We're discussing our daughter," Matthew said.

"Oh." Maryanna nodded. "Susie and I were discussing a get-together. We want to go on a camping trip. What do you think? We can invite Josh and Annie too."

Jonathan smiled at Matthew. "Sounds good to me. Matt?"

"How long did you have in mind? We've got work." Matthew looked at his wife.

"Could you take off a Friday? We can leave early and spend all day there, then spend the night and come home in the evening," Maryanna said.

"The *kinner* would love it," Jonathan added.

Maryanna smirked. "The *kinner*, huh?"

"I wouldn't mind taking my fishing pole." Matthew smiled.

"Then it's all set. I'll tell Susie and Annie, and we can figure out a date that works around everybody's schedule." Maryanna marched back into the Fisher residence to share the news with her sister.

CHAPTER TWO

"So, what do you think of Luke Beiler?" Mattie's brow rose.

Elisabeth frowned and turned off the path to pick a few wildflowers. "What do you mean?"

"Oh, don't pretend you haven't noticed!"

"Noticed what?" She brought an unknown orange blossom to her nostrils.

"Are you serious? You really haven't?"

"Mattie, I don't have a clue what you're talking about."

"Luke Beiler likes you."

She threw a red clover blossom at her friend. "He does not!"

"I can't *believe* you haven't noticed."

"Why would you think that? Don't you dare tease me like that! You know I've always thought he was handsome."

Mattie bent down and plucked a few to add to Elisabeth's growing bouquet. "The last singing I went to with you, I saw him looking our way. Or, more specifically, at you."

"You haven't been to one of our singings in over two months."

"And when we stopped and bought that watermelon from their stand the other day, he couldn't take his eyes off you."

"Really?" Elisabeth shook her head. "No way. I don't think he does."

"Lis! Yes, he most definitely does." Mattie nodded. "I'm surprised he hasn't asked you for a ride home yet."

"I think you're *ferhoodled*."

"You just wait and see; he'll ask you." Mattie loved teasing her friend and watching the color rush to her cheeks. Even she agreed that Luke Beiler was a pretty nice-looking Amish guy, and he seemed kind. "Oh, no! Now you're going to start courting Luke Beiler and you'll never come to New York!"

"First of all, Luke and I *aren't* courting. And, even if we were, I wouldn't let *him* keep me from visiting you."

"You say that now, but wait until you're all in love with him. Promise me you'll at least come visit!" Mattie knew she sounded desperate, but she couldn't imagine never seeing her best friend again.

"Are you sure you're leaving? I wish you'd stay."

"I've made up my mind. I don't want to be stuck here forever. And I know that if I meet someone here, I will be. I want to see New York. Who knows? Maybe I'll hate it and come back someday."

"No, you'll love it. I know you will." Elisabeth placed the finished bouquet into the basket that swung on her arm and smiled with pleasure.

"Promise you'll visit me?"

"I can't promise, because I don't know the future. But I will if I can, okay?"

"I guess I'll have to settle for that then." She reached over and embraced her friend. "I'm going to miss you."

"*Jah*, I'll miss you too, Mattie." Elisabeth removed a blossom from her basket and placed it into her friend's hair.

"Elisabeth, will you take these eggs over to Chloe? She and Rachel will be baking tomorrow and she asked if we had any extra to spare."

"Yes, *Mamm*. You don't think she'll mind if Mattie comes with me?"

"Of course not. And tell Chloe to stop by and say hello sometime." Leah turned from the stove and smiled.

"Okay, *Mamm*, I will."

"Mattie, will you be staying for dinner?" Leah asked.

"No. I have to be at work by one." Mattie frowned, still wondering how she would get there without her car. "Thanks for the pumpkin roll and coffee, Leah."

"Did you like it? Rachel Brenneman brought that over the other day."

"Rachel's great at baking," Elisabeth added.

"I agree," Mattie said.

"You girls have a good time," Leah called as they walked out.

Mattie turned to Elisabeth. "I like your mom; she's nice."

"So is your *mamm*."

"Most of the time. But she's been getting on my nerves lately. She sides with my dad too much."

Elisabeth's eyes widened. "Isn't that what wives are supposed to do? He's the leader of the home."

Mattie shrugged. "I guess, but I feel like Mom used to support me more. I felt like she could understand better because she used to be an *Englischer*, you know?"

"But your *vadder* was Amish."

"Yes. Maybe I should just be happy that *we're* not Amish. No offense to you. There are a lot of good things in the Amish, but I don't think I'd be able to go along with everything. I can't imagine not being able to have a car or a telephone."

"It's not so bad when you're used to it. When you don't really know about those things, it's easier to live without them. I think those who join the Amish have the hardest time because they've used worldly things their whole lives."

"Do you think a car and cell phone are worldly?"

"I don't know."

"I would think that if the leaders *really* thought they were worldly, they wouldn't use them at all. Yet, they hire drivers to take them places and have phone shanties to make calls. To me, that doesn't make any sense."

"It's just our way. Your folks don't have a television."

"I know. They value family time. And it's difficult to have time with family if everyone is staring at a screen the whole time. But I think that televisions can be used for good or for bad. Not all shows are bad."

"It's just an extra safeguard, that's all." Elisabeth turned to Mattie. "Will *you* have a television when you move to New York?"

"Maybe. But it's definitely not high on my priority list. Besides, I think I'll be so busy there I don't know if I'll find time to even watch it."

Elisabeth knocked on the back door of the Brenneman's home. She heard the sound of power tools coming from their large woodshop and figured Saul and one of his sons were probably building a new playset for a customer. She noticed a vehicle parked out by the shop.

"Hello, Elisabeth. Mattie," Chloe greeted with a smile.

"There's a truck out by the shop," Elisabeth said.

"*Jah*. Probably one of Saul's customers, no doubt." Chloe glanced toward the shop. "*Denki* for bringing these over, girls. Would you like to come in for a snack?"

"Oh, no thank you. I have to be at work at one," Mattie said.

Rachel walked up behind her mother, wearing an apron and a smile. "Mattie, will you be at the singing Sunday night?"

"I don't know. I'll see if I can get away."

"Are you and Jacob going, Lis?" Rachel's eyes sparkled.

"I will, but I can't answer for Jacob," Elisabeth said. She noticed Rachel's excitement dwindle a little.

"We'd better get going, Lis," Mattie said.

Elisabeth agreed and they turned to go.

"Tell your *Mamm* I'll see her at meeting on Sunday," Chloe called out.

"Oh," Elisabeth hollered back, "*Mamm* said to tell you to stop by sometime."

"Okay. Tell her maybe next week."

Mattie slid off the back of the motorcycle. "Thanks for the ride, Johnny."

He smiled. "That's what cousins are for, *ain't so*?"

"Sure."

"Hey, are you going to be able to get off work for the camping trip?"

"Camping trip? When?"

"Your folks ain't said nothin' to ya yet?"

Mattie frowned. "No."

"Well, yous and us and the Hostettlers are supposed to go camping soon."

Mattie's eyebrows rose. "*All* the Hostettlers?"

"*Nee*. Uncle Josh's family only."

"When?" How could her parents not have told her yet?

"A couple weeks, I think." Johnny began backing up the bike when he noticed her father approaching.

Mattie began walking to the house.

Her father nodded. "Johnny. Thanks for bringing Mattie home."

"*Gern gheschen*, Uncle Matthew."

"She won't be riding with you tomorrow."

Mattie spun around. "Yes, I will, Johnny."

"You're not allowed to ride motorcycles, in case you have forgotten." He frowned at Mattie.

"In case *you* have forgotten, I don't have a car to get to work." Mattie's planted her hand on her hip.

"Go to your room, Mattie." He turned to Johnny. "You're not to give my daughter any more rides. Is that understood?"

"Yes, Uncle Matt."

"Tell your brother too."

"All right."

Mattie slammed the door on her way into the house. "He makes me so mad!"

Maryanna walked from the kitchen into the living area where Mattie was. "What's wrong, Mattie?"

"Everything, that's what. First, Dad takes my keys, and now he's forbidden Johnny and Judah to give me a ride. What does he expect me to do? Walk four miles to work?" Mattie vented.

"I thought I told you to go to your room." Mattie turned at her father's voice.

"Mom's talking to me."

"*Now*, Matilda!"

Mattie ran up the stairs and slammed the door to her bedroom. She wished it had a lock on it. She opened her closet door and reached for an old coffee can she'd decorated two years ago. She removed the lid and dumped out the money she'd been saving. She started organizing the bills by denomination and began counting. *Five hundred dollars.* It wasn't a whole lot, but it was a start.

Oh, how she wished it were five thousand dollars! If it were five thousand, her parents would surely find her bedroom empty by tomorrow morning. But the amount was far from it. Tomorrow she'd have to ask her boss if he could give her more hours. If she didn't make more money, she'd never be able to leave. That would certainly drive her crazy.

CHAPTER THREE

"Well, he finally did it."

Mattie's brow rose at her friend's unreadable expression. "You're being elusive, Lis. Who did what?"

"Luke asked me – well, actually, he asked Jacob – if I'd ride home with him." Elisabeth nibbled her bottom lip, a half-smile on her face.

"And?"

"I did."

"And?"

Elisabeth shrugged. "It was fine."

"Fine? Just fine? Details, please."

"He seems nice. And he's cute."

"What did you talk about?"

"He talked about his work on his father's farm. He said he wants his own farm someday."

"Sounds like he's making plans."

"He is. He already has some money saved up for it."

"It sounds like he's ambitious."

Elisabeth nodded.

"Did he kiss you?"

Her friend turned two shades darker.

"I'll take that as a yes. So he *is* ambitious." Mattie grinned. "Did you kiss him back?"

"He only kissed my cheek."

"Did he ask to take you home again?"

"*Jah*."

"What did you say?"

"I said I would."

"Does this mean you're planning to stay Amish?"

Elisabeth sighed. "I'm sure I don't know what I want."

"Well, I hope you don't make any commitments until you've visited New York first."

"I haven't made any commitments. Luke and I just rode together once. But I don't know how I'd ever get all the way to New York."

"You leave that to me. Just promise me that you won't marry Luke – or anyone else – until you've had a chance to see what a different life would look like."

"Mattie, it would be a long time before I would even consider anything like getting married. I don't think you have anything to worry about."

"You and I both know these things can happen fast, Lis."

"*Nee*, I'm not ready to marry yet. Besides, I will have to be baptized first, remember? And I'm not sure I want to join the church yet."

"There's always time later if you change your mind, right? Once you join, you'll be stuck."

"I know. That's why I plan to take things slowly."

Mattie nodded. "I'm glad to hear you say that."

"I have to admit, though, New York does sound a little frightening." Elisabeth grimaced. "And fun." She smiled.

"It does, doesn't it?" She grasped her friend's arm and squeezed. "Just think of all the things there are to do there. I can't wait to go to a Broadway show."

Elisabeth frowned, her expression clueless.

"It's like a big play, or like seeing a movie in person, kind of."

"Like the Sight 'n Sound Theatre?"

"Yes, but even bigger." Mattie smiled.

"But that costs a lot of money, *jah*?"

"It's not cheap, but I hope to get a good job. It's definitely not something I'll do every week, or every month, even. Maybe I'll meet some handsome rich guy and he'll take me."

Elisabeth shook her head and grinned. "Maybe. You're *really* going to New York, aren't you?"

"Have I talked about anything else for the last year?"

"I know. It just makes me sad to know that someday you might not be here anymore."

"Don't be. I fully intend to rope you into going with me. I just wish that you and I were the same age. That would make everything so much easier."

"I don't know how my folks will ever let me go with you."

Mattie's eyes bulged. "You're going to *ask* your parents? That's not a good idea, Lis."

"Why ever not?"

"Think about it. Do you really think *your* father will give you his blessing? He won't approve any more than *my* dad will. And what do you think your mom will say?"

"You're right. So, you think that I should just leave without telling anybody?"

Mattie nodded.

Elisabeth blew out a breath. "I don't know if I'd ever have enough nerve to do that."

"When the time comes, you will." Mattie locked eyes with Elisabeth and realized she was not only speaking the words to her friend, but to herself, as well.

Rachel clung to Jacob Schrock's waist as the horse leaped over the blue barrel in the field. His male scent filled her senses as she reluctantly released her grasp.

"I'm sorry, Rachel. I should've warned you the jump was comin' up." Jacob briefly glanced back at her.

"It's okay. I saw it." She blushed, thankful Jacob couldn't see her face. "Sorry for holdin' you so tight." A strand of her blonde hair escaped from under her kerchief.

"No, it was *gut*. Uh, I mean, I'm just glad you didn't fall," he hastily added.

"Rachel!" Her mother's voice echoed in the distance.

"*Ach*, that's my *mamm*. I better go!"

"Already?" Was Jacob disappointed?

"*Jah*, I'd better."

He turned the mare around and headed toward the pasture fence that bordered their property. "You wanna ride again later?"

"I don't know. I'll have to see. Uh, you can let me off here." Rachel slid down from the saddle.

Jacob frowned. "Okay."

Rachel turned to leave as Jacob moved to release the mare from her saddle. He'd always preferred to ride bareback, so she figured he'd saddled the horse for her benefit. As soon as Rachel was out of Jacob's sight, she set out in a sprint toward home. *Dear God, please don't let*

Mamm know I was ridin' with Jacob. Rachel didn't know the reason her mother was so adamant about not riding horses. After all, she'd heard her mother and friends used to race each other all the time. Why couldn't she enjoy the same pleasure? Of course, she knew that riding with Jacob Schrock was something altogether different.

She slowed her pace as she approached the back door. "I'm here, *Mamm.*" Rachel looked around the kitchen and discovered the younger *kinner* had already returned from school. She'd finished earlier this year, the same as Jacob had. Now, she mostly stayed home to help *Mamm* out.

"Oh, *gut.* You're back." Her mother smiled.

"Did you want me to do somethin', *Mamm*?" She hoped the blush on her cheeks didn't give her away.

"Let's start on supper. We'll make your *dat's* favorite." Her mother's smile rapidly transformed into a frown. "Your dress…were you riding again?"

Rachel looked down at her dress. Sure enough, she'd managed to acquire a two-inch tear just above the hem. She chided herself. It must've happened when she squeezed through the fence between their property and the Schrocks'. "*Mamm,* I–"

"I see our girl's back." Rachel sighed in relief as her father walked through the door. Until he noticed her mother's frown. "What's wrong?"

Rachel spoke softly, "I was riding again." She absentmindedly smoothed her apron.

Her mother studied her father, waiting for what Rachel hoped wouldn't be a reprimand.

Her father frowned. "Chloe, we should let her ride *once* in a while, don't you think? Don't you remember how much you used to enjoy riding?"

"You know how I feel about this, Saul." Her mother's voice held a familiar tone. This had long been a subject of contention in their home. "I wish you'd never taught her to ride."

"But she loves horses. And everyone should know how to ride a horse," her father replied.

"I disagree. They're dangerous."

Rachel had heard this conversation before. This was the part where her mother mentioned her older sister, Amanda Chloe, who'd been injured on a horse as a girl. Even now, as a married woman with several children, she still walked with a slight limp. Rachel often wondered if her mother blamed herself for her sister's accident.

"Amanda Chloe's accident wasn't your fault, Chloe," her father's tone softened.

Rachel turned away when her father stepped close to her mother. It wasn't appropriate for the children to watch while the adults were showing affection, *Mamm* had once told her.

She couldn't decipher what her parents were whispering, but figured it was probably none of her business.

She moved toward the cupboard to retrieve the items needed for the evening meal. Rachel glanced up when her father sidled up to her.

"What I'm more concerned about is whether our daughter was riding alone or not." Her father's knowing tone caused Rachel's cheeks to flush.

Her mother gasped. "Rachel?"

"I, uh, well, Jacob Schrock asked me if I'd like to ride with him." She licked her lips. "He's a really *gut* rider, *Mamm*."

Her parents exchanged a look.

"What do you mean *with* him?" It was her father speaking now, his voice more stern than a few moments prior.

"Were you on *the same* horse? Together?" Her mother's tone indicated she was definitely in hot water.

Rachel's heartbeat quickened. She nodded. "We were just riding."

"*How* were you *just* riding?" Her father raised a brow.

Were her folks *really* asking these embarrassing questions? Their silence indicated they were waiting for her answer. She'd loved the feel of her arms wrapped around Jacob's waist and her cheek pressed against his warm back, but thinking about it now with her folks here was horrifying. She had the feeling that Jacob enjoyed it too, because he'd leaned back slightly and told her she could hold him tighter if necessary.

"Rachel?" Her father clearly required an answer.

"*Dat*, you know I like riding," she protested, hoping her parents would stop asking so many questions. It wasn't working, by her father's frown. She'd better just confess, lest she get herself into deeper trouble. "Jacob had a saddle. I was behind him, holding on."

"You weren't in a saddle?" her mother's voice rose. Many people rode without saddles in their community, but her mother's concern for safety seemed to be all-consuming.

"*Jah*, *Mamm*. I was, too. With Jacob." She took a deep breath.

"So…you were *both* in the *same* saddle," her *dat* said flatly. "Oh, boy."

"But Jacob didn't mind," Rachel assured.

"I bet he didn't." Her father frowned.

"What's wrong?" Rachel knew she wasn't supposed to be riding, but why were her folks making such a big deal out of this?

"It's not appropriate for you to ride like that, Rachel. I think you know that. And Jacob shouldn't have asked you to ride with him." Her father's gaze pierced hers. "Maybe I should go and have a word with his folks…or him."

"Oh, *Dat*! Please don't." She couldn't think of anything more humiliating.

"You're never to ride with Jacob again," her mother insisted.

Never? "But, *Mamm*–"

"You heard your mother." Her father agreed?

Tears welled up in Rachel's eyes and she fled to her bedroom. Just when she and Jacob were beginning to build a relationship, she had to cut it off? How was that fair? She'd had a crush on him for a year now. It seemed like he was *finally* beginning to notice her; at least, it felt like it.

Her folks didn't know that this was actually the third time she and Jacob had ridden together. The first time, they'd gone down to the pond and walked by the shore. The time after that, they'd gone on a picnic. This time, they'd just enjoyed the wind in their hair and conversation.

CHAPTER FOUR

He's here! Rachel discreetly watched Jacob from across the table. Although he was about ten chairs away, she still had a pretty good view of him. He laughed and talked with Luke Beiler, who'd been courting his sister, Elisabeth. It seemed the two of them had a pretty good relationship.

Jacob glanced her way then quickly turned back. Would he ask to give her a ride home tonight? She wouldn't think about it. If she did, she'd be way too nervous.

Technically, Jacob wasn't even supposed to be there tonight. If one of the chaperones spotted him and realized his age, he may be asked to leave. But it seemed most chaperones in their district tended to turn a blind eye on minor issues. Since he was only fifteen, he wasn't allowed to attend singings for another year. Rachel didn't think that was fair, since the girls were allowed to attend at fourteen. Their district was the only one she knew of that practiced this custom and she often wondered why. All of the other Amish churches around only allowed attendance at sixteen. So perhaps Jacob wouldn't be asking anyone for a ride home tonight.

Rachel sighed and turned toward Elisabeth and Mattie, who seemed to be deep in conversation. Since Mattie's family was related to several families in their district, she occasionally visited their singings. Mattie's Mennonite district had hymn sings as well, but they included the entire family – not only the young folks and a few chaperones, like their Amish community.

She'd caught Jacob's eye briefly and smiled when they'd played softball out in the Millers' field earlier, hoping he would realize that she was interested – if perchance he should ask. At the same time, she didn't wish to be too obvious.

What would it be like to ride home next to Jacob Schrock in his buggy? Rachel closed her eyes, imagining what the future might hold.

"Oh, no. My dad is so going to kill me." Mattie looked over at Johnny and Judah, who were currently being handcuffed by two police officers.

"Sorry, Mattie," Johnny said with a grimace.

"Our *dat* won't be too thrilled none either," Judah added.

Mattie scoffed. "*Your dat*? He won't do anything. He'll probably pat you on the back."

Both of the young men shook their heads adamantly. "No, he'll be upset. Especially when *Mamm* finds out. He don't like *Mamm* to cry none."

"Aunt Susie lets Uncle Jonathan get away with whatever he wants."

"Nope. That ain't true. *Dat* would get into a lot more mischief without *Mamm*."

"I knew I shouldn't have come with you guys."

"We were the ones who did it, Mattie. You shouldn't get in trouble none."

"I was driving the getaway car!"

"But you didn't know."

"Yeah, well, try explaining that to my father." Mattie frowned. "And I just got my keys back! I'm going to be grounded forever," she groaned.

"He won't tell your *dawdi*, will he?" Johnny's eyes widened.

"Oh, no. Why did you have to mention *Dawdi* Sabastian?" Mattie began to shake. "No, they're not on speaking terms. But I'm quite certain that he *will* find out somehow. And, of course, he'll blame my father for leaving the Amish. And then my parents will get into an argument. And then they'll yell at me."

"Doesn't your *Englisch* grandpa work for the police or something? Can't he get us out of this?" Judah asked.

"Officer Douglas? He's not really my grandpa. And I doubt it. We might have a better chance with Officer Love."

Both young men shook their heads. "*Nee*, we'd be worse off then."

"What about *Dawdi* Judah? You guys won't be shunned or anything, will you?" Mattie thought about her maternal grandfather, the bishop of the twins' Amish district. He also happened to be the twins' grandfather.

"*Nee*. You gotta be a baptized member to be shunned," Johnny said.

"Did they tell you what's going to happen? Do we have to stay here?" Mattie frowned.

"I think they'll hold us until someone comes to get us out. I wonder if they'll have to pay money," Judah said.

"I hope not. If my Dad has to pay, he'll make me pay him back."

"Don't worry, Mattie. We can help pay too."

The boys' offer was kind, but brought little comfort. What on earth would her father say to her this time? She would almost rather stay in jail.

"Well, Mattie, what do you have to say for yourself?" Maryanna huffed.

She looked at her mother in disillusionment. Usually, Mom would be the first to come to her rescue when Dad was giving her the evil eye. "Mom, I was innocent!"

"I think you need to look up the definition of innocent. Because it seems that yours doesn't match ours – or the law's. There's a good reason your car is impounded for thirty days. Which *you* are paying for, by the way." Her father's glare brought little comfort.

Oh, no! If she had to pay for her car, how would she ever get enough money to go to New York? "How much will it cost?"

"I'm guessing about thirty dollars per day."

"For *thirty* days?" her voice screeched. "But that's…that's like nine hundred dollars."

"Yeah. Maybe you should have thought about that *before* you became partner to a crime."

"It wasn't really that bad, Dad. You make us sound like criminals. JJ just thought it would be fun to get some fireworks. And, in my defense, I didn't know they hadn't paid for them."

"I would think the two of them running to the car and telling you to step on the gas would have been a clue." Her father rubbed his forehead. "And it *is* a big deal. When are you going to realize that you are going down the wrong path? What's it going to take for you to wake up? You were arrested, Matilda!"

She absolutely hated when her father used her full name. She loved her paternal great grandmother for whom she was named, but she much preferred Mattie for herself.

"Dad, it was all just a big misunderstanding. You see, Johnny thought that Judah had already paid for the fireworks, and Judah thought that Johnny had paid for them."

"And the officers believed that explanation? That's surprising." He crossed his arms over his chest then turned to her mother. "Maybe we should sell her car, Maryanna."

"*Sell* my car?" Tears welled in Mattie's eyes. "What are you going to do, Dad? Keep me locked in my room for the rest of my life?"

He frowned. "I'm considering that option. At least it would keep you out of jail."

She knew her father didn't really mean it. He was just venting, as he often did when they argued. "I have a job, Dad." She hoped reminding him of that fact would make him realize that she was indeed responsible.

"Which you are going to lose, if you keep up this behavior."

"I get it, okay?"

"Do *not* use that tone of voice with me. Sometimes I think it would have been better if we had stayed Amish."

"Oh no, not this again." Mattie rolled her eyes. "Johnny and Judah are Amish, and they're the ones who got me in trouble, Dad. Being Amish doesn't help them any." The last thing she needed was *more* restrictions!

"Mattie, go to your room!"

"I've got to work tomorrow."

"Now!"

Mattie hastily turned and marched to her room. It was times like this she wished Elisabeth had a cell phone too. Surely her friend had already heard about her and JJ being locked up. The Amish grapevine tended to spread news quicker than the daily newspaper. She wondered what, if anything, would happen to Jonathan and Judah.

"Mattie."

Mattie rolled over on her bed and glanced at her alarm clock. Was it six o'clock already? Apparently, she'd fallen asleep.

"Mattie, it's time for supper," her sister Rebekah called from the other side of her door. "You'd better come before Dad comes up here."

Mattie groaned and rolled out of bed.

"By the way, *Dawdi* Judah and *Mammi* Lydia are here."

"I'm coming." She looked out her window in search of a horse and buggy near the barn. Sure enough, her grandparents were there. Although her maternal grandparents were Amish and her grandfather was the bishop, they seemed much less strict than her paternal grandparents. Mattie would have looked forward to spending time with her grandparents, had she not been in hot water. Hopefully, her father would act civilized.

She quickly smoothed out her dress, but left her hair down, and quickly trotted downstairs. The moment her feet hit the bottom step, she caught her father's look of disapproval.

"Mattie." Her father approached her in short order. "Why is your hair down?"

"Rebekah said to hurry, and I didn't feel like putting it up."

"You didn't *feel* like putting it up?" Her father frowned.

She knew she was defying her father, but he's the one who'd wanted her to hurry. How could she hurry *and* fix her hair? Why did she have to follow her father's nonsensical rules anyway? What did it matter if she wore her hair up or down, covered or uncovered? "Maybe I want to wear it down."

"You won't in *this* house. Go back to your room and don't come back down until your hair is up." He pointed to her room. "And covered."

Mattie resisted the urge to argue with her father and did as told. She wouldn't contest, for the sake of her grandparents visiting. If they hadn't been there, though, she would have asked her father why she couldn't wear her hair down. Funny, she'd never thought to ask before.

Several moments later, Mattie walked into the dining area with her hair pinned up and her head covering in place. She rushed to give her grandparents a hug before her father had a chance to criticize anything else.

"Take a seat, Mattie," her father ordered.

She joined the others at the table, then bowed her head to pray. As soon as her father finished the blessing, she felt his stare on her.

"What?" She lifted her gaze to her father's.

"You know you're not allowed to wear color on your lips. Please take it off."

If it's not one thing, it's another. Mattie frowned, but she took her napkin and removed her lip gloss.

"Thank you."

"Well, look at all this delicious food!" Her grandfather smiled and passed a plate of mashed potatoes to her brother. "Who made it?"

"All us girls, 'cept Mattie. She was in trouble."

Mattie frowned at her youngest sister. "You don't need to gossip, Ellie. Keep your mouth closed."

"Mattie!" Her mother gasped.

"Just eat, girls," Matthew reprimanded. He looked at his father-in-law. "I apologize, Judah. We've been dealing with *issues* lately."

"He means *me*," Mattie volunteered.

"Not now, Mattie," Maryanna warned.

"I heard you and the twins encountered trouble," her grandfather spoke.

"Mattie was in jail, *Dawdi Judah*!" Ellie volunteered.

"Ellie, I told you to keep your mouth shut! Mind your own beeswax." Sometimes Mattie felt like taking some tape and sticking it over her sister's mouth.

"It's true. I heard Daddy tellin' Mom," she insisted.

Her mother spoke up, "Ellie, sometimes it's better not to repeat things we hear. Especially when it's about someone else."

"Even if it's true?" Ellie protested.

"Yes, Ellie, even if it's true. It's best just not to say anything," Maryanna said.

Ellie shook her head. "It's hard not to say anything."

Her grandfather chuckled. "I agree with you there." He winked at Ellie.

"Let's just eat now, and we can talk later. How does that sound?" Her grandmother Lydia had always tried to be a peacekeeper. "Judah?"

Judah smiled at her grandmother. "That sounds good to me. I think I'd like to have some time with my oldest granddaughter after supper." He winked at Mattie.

"She's not really the oldest," Ellie said.

"Well, she's the oldest in *this* family," her grandfather said.

"Want to talk about it?"

Mattie's brow lifted as she made eye contact with her grandfather. "Not really."

"That's okay. We can just–"

"My dad makes me so angry sometimes! He blames me for everything, even when it isn't my fault."

"I see." He rubbed his white beard.

"He expects me to be responsible, yet he doesn't even offer to give me a ride to work. How does he expect me to do that?"

"I could loan you one of my buggies."

Mattie grimaced. "No, thank you, *Dawdi* Judah."

He reached over and grasped her hand. His kind eyes met hers. “Matilda, no one, besides *Der Herr*, will ever love you more than your folks do.”

“Well, they sure don’t act like it. And will you *please* only call me Mattie, *Dawdi*?”

He nodded. “Don’t they, Mattie?” His brow rose.

“All they want to do is take away everything I have. My car, my job, my friends, my freedom.”

“Why?”

“I don’t know. Because they want to make my life miserable?”

“I don’t know of any parents who want their children to be miserable. Perhaps they’re just trying to protect you.”

“From what?”

“There are a lot of things out in the world that can hurt you. There are people who’ll take advantage of you. I advise you to listen to your folks. They may not be right about everything, but, I can assure you, they only want your best. They love you.”

“Well, they have a lousy way of showing it.”

“Parents don’t always do what’s right; that’s true. But *your* responsibility is to obey them.”

“I’ve tried. Nothing I do makes them happy.”

“You don’t believe that, do you?”

“It seems like it.”

"How can we resolve this issue?"

Mattie shook her head. "I don't know. I sometimes think Mom and Dad might be happier if I weren't here."

Judah grasped his granddaughter's hand. "Matil-Mattie, don't ever think that. They only want what's best for you."

Tears pricked her eyes. "Then why are they making my life so difficult?"

"You are so blessed. I wish you could see that."

"Well, I don't feel like it."

"There are billions of people without half of what you have. Some people don't even have a place to live or food to eat. You are blessed, Mattie."

"I understand all that, and I feel sorry for those people, but *this* is *my* reality. Everybody has their problems. I know I have more blessings than some, but having things isn't what life is about."

His forehead rose. "What do you think life is all about?"

"It's about being happy. It's about living your life the way *you* want to live it – not how someone else wants you to."

"I disagree."

"Well, you're Amish because you choose to be. My folks are Mennonite because that's how they want to be. But what about me? When do I get to decide to choose what *I* want?"

"I have chosen to stay Amish – that is true. But my choice wasn't about what *I* wanted, it was what I felt God wanted. When we agreed on a New Order way back when your folks were just youngsters, it was a big decision – one that many didn't agree with and left the church over. We lost many friends.

"But when Gideon Fisher came to me with Bible Truth that I could not refute, I realized that I had to swallow my pride, admit that I and others before me had been wrong, and acknowledge the Truth. I believe everyone comes to that moment at some point in their life. Some call it 'The Valley of Decision'. Oftentimes, the most important decisions are the most difficult to make – for, your future and the future of the generations that come after you, hinges on the outcome of those decisions.

"If others in this community didn't agree with what I came to know as the Truth, I wouldn't be here today. In fact, I'd probably be *Englisch*." He chuckled. "Imagine your *grossdawdi* as an *Englischer*."

Mattie smiled, envisioning her Amish grandfather in *Englisch* clothing and driving a car.

"Whatever you choose, Mattie, choose wisely." He patted her hand. "Come now, let's go try some of that homemade ice cream your *grossmudder* made."

CHAPTER FIVE

"I know I'm never going to get out of here, Lis!" Sometimes Mattie felt sorry for her friend always having to hear her vent. She felt like breaking down and sobbing.

"Maybe you should stop trying."

"I hope you're joking." Mattie sighed. "I'm going to lose my mind soon. I know I will."

"No, you won't." Elisabeth smiled. "I think the best way for you to be able to go to New York is for you to stop stressing out about it so much. Enjoy where God has you right now. What if you don't ever go to New York? Then your whole life will be wasted on a dream that was never fulfilled."

"Please don't say that, Lis. I can't give up my dream."

"That's not what I'm saying. I'm saying that I think you should stop trying so hard. Mattie, all you ever talk about is New York. You still have a life here. Now. Cherish what you've been given every moment of your life. You never know when those things might be snatched away from you. I think we often take our blessings for granted."

"Okay, I think I understand what you're saying."

"Enjoy life now. And when the time is right for you to go to New York, the doors will open wide for you and you will walk through them."

"Do you think so?"

"I know so." Elisabeth smiled. "Come to the singing with me."

"Okay."

"Really? You will?"

"Did you just squeal? I don't think I've ever heard you do that."

Elisabeth shrugged. "I don't know."

"Are you and Luke Beiler going to make goo-goo eyes at each other all night?"

"Goo-goo eyes?" Elisabeth giggled. "I think Luke would laugh at that."

"You're not going to try to fix me up with anyone, right? Because I do not want a relationship right now. And it would be unfair to him. You know I would never become Amish."

"Of course not. I just want you to have a good time. You like to play volleyball and baseball, don't you?"

"You know I do."

"Mattie, are your things packed? We need to load everything in the car," Maryanna called from the bottom of the stairs.

"No. I'm not going."

"What do you mean, you're not going?" Maryanna sighed and frowned at Matthew as he walked in.

"What's wrong? Why the long face? We're going camping. You should be excited." Matthew smiled and kissed her cheek.

If only she could share his enthusiasm. If only she didn't have to ruin his happy moment. It seemed when he and Mattie were near each other, those moments were few and far between.

"Mattie says she's not going," she said flatly.

"Mattie needs to realize that she's not the one in charge. Don't worry about it, *schatzi.* We're going to have a great, relaxing time. I'll talk to her." Matthew walked to the stairs and hollered, "Mattie, get your stuff ready and put it in the van."

"I'm not going. I have to work," she called.

Matthew looked at Maryanna. "Where's her boss' phone number?"

"On the fridge."

He walked to the fridge with his cell phone in hand. “Hello, Mr. Watson, this Mattie Riehl’s father. She’ll be out of town this weekend, beginning today, so you’ll have to find a replacement for her. I’m sorry about the inconvenience. Thank you; I appreciate it. Goodbye.”

Matthew walked back to the stairs. “Let’s go, Mattie. You’re not working this weekend after all.”

“What?” Mattie’s tone was sharp.

“You heard me. No work this weekend. Get ready to go.”

“But I asked Mr. Watson for more hours.”

“He’s finding someone else to work your shifts. Hurry up. We’re leaving in fifteen minutes.”

“I don’t want to go.”

“Too bad. You’re going whether you want to or not. Now, if you don’t want to spend the entire weekend in the outfit you’re wearing, I suggest you pack quickly.”

Maryanna heard Mattie sigh in protest. A moment later, activity upstairs suggested Mattie had begun packing her things for the trip. Perhaps this would be a pleasant vacation after all.

Matthew pounded a tent stake into the ground and glanced up to see Mattie walking toward the Fishers’ campsite. “Mattie, I don’t want you going anywhere until all the tents are set up. If your girls' tent is finished, please help the boys with theirs."

Mattie clenched her hands then began walking back to her younger siblings' tent.

"Matthew, will you build a fire in the pit?" Maryanna asked, holding sticks the children had gathered earlier for roasting marshmallows and hotdogs. "We should probably sharpen these too."

"In just a little bit, *schatzi.* I've gotta get this tent up." Matthew smiled.

Jonathan Fisher approached. "Yep, then you two can do some smoochin'."

"Wanna give me a hand with this?" Matthew raised a brow to Jonathan.

"Sure. Josh, come help us out!" Jonathan hollered.

Joshua Hostettler walked into their camping space. "Do you have another hammer or a hatchet?"

"Over by that stack of firewood." Matthew pointed in the direction of the fire pit.

Joshua promptly began pounding one of the tent stakes with the blunt end of the hatchet. "We should really do this more often."

"We should. The children love it," Jonathan agreed.

All three of the men looked up when Mattie hollered, "Thomas, get over here and help me with your tent!"

"Well, *most* of them do," Matthew said.

"Mattie will have a great time too; you'll see. She just doesn't know it yet," Joshua encouraged.

"I hope so. And I pray she doesn't drive her mother and me crazy." Matthew sighed.

"I've certainly driven my mother crazy a time or two." Jonathan grinned.

"A time or two? Jonathan, you *still* drive your mother crazy. And probably poor Susie too." Matthew stood up and attempted to piece together the tent poles.

"*Ach*, who wants a boring life? Fun people are the ones who are remembered the most," Jonathan asserted.

"Yeah, well, I'd like to be remembered for the good things I've done," Joshua added.

"All done!" Matthew proclaimed. "Do you guys have your tents set up already?"

"Yep!" Jonathan said.

"Sure do." Joshua smiled.

"Great! Let's do some fishing." Matthew beamed.

Mattie walked alongside Johnny and Judah as they rode their scooters through the campground. "I wish I'd brought my bike with me."

"You can ride my scooter," Judah offered.

"No, it's okay. I don't mind walking too much. I'm just glad the lake's not very far."

"The water's gonna feel great!" Johnny proclaimed.

Mattie moved to the side when she heard a vehicle approaching, and alerted JJ.

"Hey, Mattie."

Mattie's jaw dropped. "Lis? What are you doing here?"

Her friend glanced to the driver's seat and smiled. "Luke wanted to go for a drive. I suggested we come here."

"Great! You're just in time to go swimming with us," Judah invited.

"Sounds like fun." Luke smiled.

"Oh." Elisabeth snapped her fingers. "I didn't bring anything to swim in."

"I've got some extra culottes in the tent. If you wanna drive back there, just ask my mom and she'll show you," Mattie said.

"Alright." Elisabeth smiled. "If Luke doesn't mind."

Luke raised a brow. "Anything for you, Elisabeth."

"We'll meet you guys at the lake in a little bit," Elisabeth said.

Mattie watched Elisabeth and her beau drive off. "Do you know if Luke has his driver's license?"

Both Johnny and Judah shook their heads.

"Do you guys have a license for your motorcycles?" Mattie smiled.

"*Jah*. Had to get one," Johnny said.

"Do you think the water will be cold?" Mattie changed the subject.

"I hope so," Judah said.

Mattie's eyes widened. "You do?"

"Yep. I love swimming in cold water!" Judah grinned.

"You're weird," Mattie teased.

He shrugged. "Get it from *Daed*, I guess."

Mattie laughed. "That, you do."

"Where's Mattie? She should have been back by now." Maryanna looked toward the darkening sky.

Matthew lifted his marshmallow stick from the flames. "I haven't seen her. Where did she say she was going?"

"Swimming with JJ, Elisabeth, and Luke."

"I thought they came back already."

"Luke and Elisabeth left, and I think JJ are at their campsite, but I don't remember seeing Mattie."

Matthew frowned. "Do you think she's with the Fishers?"

"We should probably check. I'll go over to Josh and Annie's; you check Jonathan and Susie's." Maryanna looked at Rebekah. "Stay here and make sure the younger ones don't get too close to the fire."

"Okay, *Mamm*," Rebekah replied.

Matthew hurried to Jonathan's campsite. "Have any of you seen Mattie?"

Jonathan, Susie, and their children all sat around the fire. Judah looked at Johnny then spoke up, "Last we saw her, she was with that guy." He looked at his brother. "What was his name?"

Johnny squinted. "Um…Darren? No, it was Derrick, I think."

"Derrick who?" Matthew asked. "Do we know him?"

JJ shook their heads. "Met him today down at the lake. Mattie went on his boat."

"And you left her there alone with him?" Matthew's heart began to pound.

Jonathan jumped up. "I'll help you look for her."

"Where did you see her last?" Matthew quizzed the boys.

"She said they were goin' for a walk," Judah said.

"Let's go," Jonathan suggested.

"We can help," Johnny offered. "I'll get our flashlights."

"Let's split up. Johnny, you come with me. Judah, stay with your dad. We'll head out toward the lake. Jonathan, do you and Judah want to scour the campground?" Matthew looked toward his family's campsite. "I'm gonna go let Maryanna know what's going on."

"We can ask Josh to help. I'm sure he wouldn't mind," Jonathan said. "I'll walk over and ask him to join us."

Matthew agreed and glanced at the time on his cell phone. "Okay. Let's meet back in a half hour."

"We can text you if we find her," one of the twins said.

Matthew nodded. "I'll do the same."

Mattie laid back on the quilt and stared up at the stars. "I've always been fascinated with the sky at night. Aren't all those stars amazing?" She smiled at the handsome young man next to her, his sandy blond hair glistening in the moonlight.

"Sure." He rubbed the sand from his tanned torso and swim trunks and took a drink from the bottle he held.

"Derrick, what's it like on the West Coast? I mean, do the stars look the same there?"

"I can't say I've noticed. I don't usually surf at night, you know. But I sure noticed you." He moved closer and wove his fingers through her hair. "I had a great time with you today, Mattie."

"Yeah, me too. You'll probably forget all about me when you go back home."

"Never," Derrick whispered. As their lips met for the countless time today, his breath smelled of the beer he'd just finished. "Mm…you could come back with me, you know. I've got a place not too far from the beach."

"The beach? I've always wanted to visit the ocean."

"Come with me, babe." He kissed her lips again. "I bet you'd look hot in a bikini."

Mattie laughed. "A bikini? I don't think so."

"Oh, I know so." His hands caressed her back and drew her even closer. "Let's go back to my tent. I think there's room in my sleeping bag for both of us."

"I don't know, Derrick. We just met."

"So. There's no reason why that should stop us. We're both old enough to know what we want." His bangs fell over his eyes.

"I'm not ready for that sort of thing."

His warm hand trailed her arm and his breath felt hot on her neck. "Come with me, Mattie. I'll show you a good time."

Matthew thought he'd heard Mattie's voice along with a young man's. He signaled to Johnny to keep silent, and they both quietly approached the lake's edge.

What on earth? He shook his head as he briefly listened in on their conversation. Right about now, he felt he could wring Mattie's neck. What was she thinking?

He flicked on the flashlight and shined the bright light in their eyes. "Oh, no you won't, buddy! Take your hands off my daughter."

Mattie's eyes widened. "Dad?"

"What do you think you're doing? Mattie, you know our dating standards." How many times had he and her mother gone over this with her? He glared at the young man next to her. "Absolutely *no* touching."

Mattie's friend's confused expression wasn't unexpected. "No touching? Like, *at all*? That's harsh, man."

"Back to the campsite, Mattie. Now!" Matthew demanded. He looked at the unscrupulous young man. "Where are your parents?"

"Dude, I'm here with my buddies. The old man's at home."

"Get lost before I do something that'll land you in the hospital and me in jail. And don't come near my daughter again."

"Chill out, man. We were just havin' a good time. I didn't mean nothin' by it." The young man reached for his shirt, but left his empty bottles on the quilt. Matthew frowned as he walked off unfazed.

"This is why dads with daughters should never carry loaded guns," Matthew mumbled under his breath. He turned to Johnny. "Text your dad and let him know we found Mattie."

"I just don't know what to do with her," Matthew vented in frustration. "I leave her alone for a few hours and then I find her with a total stranger, and he...he..." He covered his eyes with his hand. "I don't even want to think about it. If I had come at a later time, if I hadn't arrived at that exact moment..." Matthew shook his head.

"*Der Herr* was watching out for her, for certain sure," Jonathan stated.

Joshua nodded in silent agreement.

"I'm just…" Matthew swallowed hard, "at a loss of what to do."

"Do what you have been doing," Joshua advised. "Discipline her. She needs to understand that negative consequences follow negative actions. It will teach her responsibility. But do it in the right spirit. Do it because you love her and want what's best for her, not because you're angry."

"I *do* love her and want what's best for her," Matthew

protested somewhat defensively.

"*We* know you do, Matt," Jonathan agreed, "but does *Mattie* know that? Sure, she and you get upset at each other, but does she *know* you love her, even though she's being punished?"

Matthew sighed. "I don't know. I think so."

"I'm not saying she shouldn't be chastised. Just be certain you do it in the right spirit. Make sure she *knows* you love her. That's important in a girl's life." Joshua nodded toward their camp. "My *fraa* can verify that. Her *daed* wasn't one for showing much affection."

Matthew digested the advice, then turned to Jonathan. "Anything you would like to add to that, Minister Fisher?"

Jonathan chuckled. "I wonder if this was what *my vadder* thought when dealing with me."

"If so, I most sincerely empathize."

"Hey!" Jonathan exclaimed in feigned offense. "Seriously, though, our children belong to *Der Herr*, Matt. They're not ours, they're His. Just do your best, pray for her, and leave her in God's hands."

Jathan eyed him warily, awaiting his response.

"I hate to say it, Jathan. But this is your own doing. You're reaping the consequences of your actions."

Jathan frowned. "But my Sarah's alive."

The bishop nodded. "And married to another man – an *Englischer*."

"But she's still *my* wife!"

"*Nee*, Jathan. She hasn't been your *fraa* for ten years."

"I still love Sarah." He hated that tears misted his eyes, especially in front of Bishop Bontrager. "Seeing her again..." His mind wandered back to Sarah, sleeping so peacefully on the couch. He'd stared at her face for a whole hour, gently stroking her fine hair while he should've been out working in the field. It had been wonderful *gut* to have her back in the house. To touch her soft face. It was almost like a dream. A wonderful dream.

"There's nothing you can do now, Jathan. You're too late." The bishop's words pulled him out of his trance.

"Why? Can't I go to the judge? Tell him she was my wife first. I can fight for her."

"And if she doesn't want to come home? Jathan, you know that is not our way." The sternness in Bishop Bontrager's voice was clear. "Besides, we don't want the *Englisch* in our business. They'll just cause trouble. I think it may have been a mistake allowing you to marry an *Englisch* woman."

"But she'd become Amish. Sarah loved me. I know she did."

"Perhaps."

"Surely, there's *something* I can do." He hated that he sounded so desperate. But he was, wasn't he?

"You can pray. You know God is the Righteous Judge. Go to Him."

"I've already done that."

"You can always pray more. He never tires of hearing from His children."

"I'm afraid God isn't listening. I've been praying for Sarah to come back for ten years now."

Bishop Bontrager's eyes widened. "And she has. It sounds as if *Gott* may be listening after all."

Jathan sipped the tea the bishop's wife had offered him earlier. "But I didn't want her to come back this way. I wanted her to come back home. Back to us."

"God's ways are not our ways."

"What does God want from me?"

"Your obedience. Your trust."

"But how can I get my Sarah back?"

"Jathan." The bishop shook his head. "It is not for us to know these things. You just pray, Jathan. Pray for *Der Herr's* will."

Just pray. Jathan thought on the bishop's words as he slapped the reins to urge Driver on. "God, aren't you tired of me prayin' the same thing by now?" he spoke the words to the air. "I know I am," he mumbled.

"How long, God? How long will my past chase me? I gave up drinkin'; You know I did. Why, then? Why can't I have my wife back?" *Pray for God's will.* "Okay, God. I'm praying for Your will, but if I could please find favor in Your eyes, I'll do my best to love her like I'm supposed to."

Jathan pulled in to the long lane at the edge of his property. Something seemed different – something felt different. He looked toward the house. A charcoal gray truck was parked in front of the house. His heart jumped within his chest. Could it be Sarah?

"Yah!" he commanded his mare. He rolled to a stop just in front of the barn. It seemed like it took two weeks just to reach the hitching post.

He slid down, not bothering to tether the horse, and hurried toward the porch.

"Sarah?" he called out, marching up the steps.

"I'm here, Jathan," her delightful voice sounded from the side porch.

Excitement filled his heart. He rounded the corner. And then came to an abrupt stop. His eyes moved to Sarah's side.

"Jathan, I'd like you to meet my husband, Mark." Sarah wore an unsure expression.

Jathan swallowed, and stared at the man's outstretched hand. There was no way he was shaking the hand of the man who stole his wife.

"Nice place you got here," the man said. He dropped his hand to his side.

Jathan frowned. He looked at Sarah. "Why did you bring him with you?"

"I wanted you two to meet."

"Why?"

"Well, because. I wanted you to believe that I *really* am married."

"You're married to me."

"I realize that." Sarah stared at her hands.

"You do?" Well, at least she admitted it now. That was certainly a step in the right direction.

"Yes. I have amnesia."

"Amnesia? What is this?"

"It means that I lost my memory."

Jathan frowned, attempting to take it all in.

The man with Sarah stepped forward. It was apparent he'd rather not be there. "Listen, Jathan. We're trying to make the best out of an awkward situation here. Sarah and I talked and agreed she could stop by once a week to spend time with the children. Are you okay with this arrangement?"

"I want my wife back!" Jathan clenched his hands at his side.

"I'm sorry, but that's not possible."

Who did this guy think he was? "Sarah, what do *you* say?" His gaze steadied on her.

"I can't come back to you, Jathan. I'm sorry. I have another life now." She reached out and briefly touched his hand. Her eyes searched his. "Would it be better for you if we got a divorce?"

"You would *divorce* me?" Pain gripped his heart at the idea that Sarah would even suggest it.

"If it would make it easier for you. I mean, you could remarry someone else."

He shook his head vigorously. "Never. We do not believe in divorce; God hates it. Even if I could remarry, I don't want to. You're the only woman I've ever wanted. I need *you*, Sarah." How could he convince her to stay and give him a second chance?

The man beside Sarah sighed, clearly becoming impatient. "Will you allow Sarah to see the children once a week, or not?"

Jathan's brow rose. Seeing Sarah once a week was better than not seeing her at all. He would take the crumbs. Maybe he could win her love again. "You would allow her to come?"

"For the *children*, yes," the man said.

"Will *you* come too?" Jathan frowned.

The man glanced at Sarah. "Sarah and I haven't discussed that yet."

"Sarah can come." He smiled at his wife. "She is welcome any time."

Sarah stepped forward. "When would be a good time?"

"Sunday after meeting would be best." He always felt he looked his best on church days. Should he invite her to attend? "We have meeting every two weeks. You – you could come, Sarah." He would ignore the whispers that would no doubt arise from the women at meeting. Who knows what rumors were already flying around the community?

She blessed Jathan with a soft smile, one he hadn't seen in entirely too long. "Thank you for the offer, Jathan. We already have a church that we attend on Sundays."

Jathan now watched as his wife drove away with another man. If only he could go back and do things differently. If only he could win her devotion again.

CHAPTER SIX

"Mattie? Is that you?"

Mattie had hoped her sisters were asleep. She settled down into her sleeping bag. "Yes, it's me, Ellie. Go to sleep."

"Where were you?"

Mattie sighed. If it wasn't a lecture from her father, it was endless questions from her little sister. "Somewhere else, and it's none of your business."

"I don't think you were supposed to go off. Mom–"

"Go to sleep, Ellie, or I'll tell Dad."

Her young sister huffed and rolled over, away from Mattie. Good. Ellie had probably decided not to speak to her now.

Mattie stared at the ceiling of the tent that she shared with her sisters and reminisced about her day with Derrick. Why did her father have to show up and ruin everything? It wasn't every day she had the opportunity to meet a handsome surfer from California. They'd been having a good time. And it wasn't like she was *actually* going to join him in his tent. She knew better than that. If only her father would back off. She was nearly an adult. Surely she should be allowed *some* freedom. What was he going to do, follow her around forever?

Mattie turned on her side, unable to rest. Her phone vibrated against her leg and she shrunk down into her sleeping bag to pull it out. A text from Judah. She read it in the privacy of her sleeping bag. *Come outside.* She wondered what mischief her cousins had planned now. She quietly got out of her sleeping bag and started for the tent exit.

"Didn't Daddy tell you to stay inside?" It was Ellie. Again.

"I have to use the bathroom. Go to sleep and quit being so nosy."

She left the tent and headed behind it when she saw the twins' forms. "What are we doing?" she whispered.

The moonlight shone off her cousins' eager expressions as they held out three rolls of toilet paper. "TP all the parents' tents?"

She grabbed a roll with an impish grin. "You bet."

The three silently sneaked toward Jonathan and Susie's tent, keeping an eye out for anyone else. They reached the small dwelling and began unrolling their toilet paper over it.

Mattie struggled to contain any giggles that might escape and ruin their plan. With their first mission accomplished, they stealthily headed back to her parents' dwelling. Mattie relished the thought of her father's bewildered expression tomorrow morning when he discovered what they'd done.

"Mattie?"

At her father's voice, Mattie whirled around and quickly hid the toilet paper roll behind her back.

"Dad? Oh, uh, what are you doing out here?" Surely her fake smile gave her away.

"I should ask you the same thing, young lady." Why were her father's hands conspicuously behind his back?

"I was just, uh, you know, out."

"No, I don't know. I'm quite certain I told you to stay in your tent. And what are you hiding behind your back?"

She frowned, reluctantly showing him her roll of toilet paper. "I, you know, had to use the outhouse."

"Outhouse?"

"Uh, restroom."

"They already have toilet paper in there."

"I know. But it doesn't hurt to be prepared, does it? You know, just in case they're out."

Her father looked past her to JJ. "Boys, what are you doing out?"

"Oh, uh, hello, Uncle Matthew," Johnny started. "*Jah*,

we had to use the outhouse too." He held out his TP and his twin did the same.

"We figured we would, um, escort Mattie there because of what happened, you know, with that Derrick guy," Judah attempted to recover. "A good idea, *ain't so*?"

Her father shook his head. "You three hurry up and do your business and then head back to your tents, you hear?" He met his Mattie's gaze. "I'll be watching for *you*."

"Okay, Dad." Mattie and JJ hurried toward the direction of the bathrooms.

Johnny glanced at Mattie. "You don't think he believed us, do you?"

"No." Mattie shook her head. "He suspects something's up. And he'll probably come looking for me if I'm not back in a few minutes." She sighed. "Well, it looks like you guys will have to finish the job without me."

"That's all right, Mattie. You can see it in the morning, *jah*?" Judah smiled.

Mattie grinned. "I sure will. Good night."

"Night," the twins echoed.

Matthew waited until Mattie was back in her tent before heading to Joshua's camp. He knew his friend would likely be asleep by now, or perhaps snuggling with his wife. In both cases, he wasn't likely to hear his mission of mischief. It had been too long since he'd been able to pull any pranks on his friends. He quietly unraveled the toilet paper and slowly walked around his friend's tent.

He had planned on including Jonathan in this undertaking, but when he'd gone to his tent, the short interchange he'd overheard between Jonathan and Susie told Matthew enough to know that his friend would be distracted for quite a while. So he was doing it alone.

Matthew grinned. Joshua would most likely assume Jonathan was to blame. He loved his relationship with his friends. You never knew what to expect.

Jonathan broke away from Susie for a moment. "*Schatzi*."

"Yes, *lieb*?" Susie met his gaze in the dim moonlight, and Jonathan tried not to dwell on how much he enjoyed the love in her voice and how her eyes strayed back to his lips.

"I've been wondering about Matthew."

She shifted and her gaze cleared some. "Mm…hmm?"

He also enjoyed the disappointment in her tone.

"He's been too serious lately about Mattie and all. I was thinkin' that we should cheer him up some."

"Wasn't that one of the main reasons we came on this

trip?"

"*Jah*. But I wanna do something better."

Susie studied his face for a moment then grinned. "What prank do you have cooked up now, *liebchen*?"

He smiled back at her. She knew him so well. "I want to TP his tent."

She gasped. "Jonathan! Do you know how? Have you ever done it before?"

"No, but I saw someone on an *Englischer's* TV once. It didn't look none too hard."

Susie turned to lie on her back and was quiet for a moment. "Are you gonna take the toilet paper from the public bathrooms?"

"*Jah,* I was plannin' on it."

Susie turned on her side and reached for him. "Jonathan?"

"Yes, *Schatzi*?"

"May I join you?"

Jonathan grinned and met her mouth with his. "I was hoping you'd say that."

Joshua smiled at his ingenious plan. It was simple: sneak to Jonathan's tent, TP it, and then get away as stealthily as possible. It would be just like old times, when they were all boys and wreaked havoc on all of Paradise. Their pranks had reduced to a minimum since they had all married, and even more as they all had children of their own. But this would be a great reminder of the good ol' days for all of them.

He also planned to TP Matthew's tent, just as soon as he was finished with Jonathan's. And his friends would likely suspect each other too. Joshua had always been the least troublemaking of the bunch, but he had a few surprises up his sleeve.

He continued to Jonathan's camp, approaching from the back side. His jaw dropped as he spotted his friend's tent. It was already covered top-to-bottom with toilet paper. Apparently, he hadn't been the only one with that idea. Matthew was up to his old antics as well. Joshua grinned and started for Matt's camp instead.

He groaned aloud when he reached Matthew's tent. It, too, was blanketed white. He had thought he'd be the only one, recreating memories and giving them all a good laugh. Apparently, he'd been a step behind.

Joshua stilled at a thought. *What if...? Oh no.* He started back for his camp at a fast walk. He paused at the sight of his tent and sighed in relief. It was untouched. Yes! No yards of trash to clean up in the morning.

He glanced down at his worthless roll of toilet paper. *Well, that hadn't worked out so well.* He quietly opened his tent and crawled in, then settled down beside Annie.

"Josh?" she murmured sleepily, pulling him closer to her and leaning her head on his shoulder.

"Mm…hmm?"

"I'm so lucky I have you."

He smiled and pressed a kiss to her forehead. "And I'm lucky to have you, sweet Annie."

"Good night, *lieb*."

"*Guten nacht*."

How could he care about a failed prank when he had a wife like Annie? Joshua snuggled in with the love of his life and closed his eyes in contentment.

"Matthew Riehl?"

Matt turned at the sound of thc deep male voice. "Yes, that's me." He eyed the park ranger, hoping he wouldn't bring up the disordered state of their campsite.

"Are you responsible for these three campsites?" The ranger showed him a map, where three boxes were circled, indicating the spaces that his family, Jonathan's family, and Joshua's family occupied.

Matthew cringed. "That's correct."

"There seemed to be a disturbance last night. I'm sure you probably noticed." The ranger rubbed his chin. "You wouldn't happen to know anything about it, would you?"

"Yes, sir. My friends and I were pulling friendly pranks on each other. We'll be sure to clean it up."

"That's all good and well, sir, but are you aware that vandalizing someone else's property, even if it is with toilet paper, is a misdemeanor? And are you also aware that taking toilet paper from a public bathroom is theft?"

Matthew swallowed. "No, I didn't realize that."

"I won't prosecute you – this time. However, let this be a warning to you for future activities."

"I appreciate that, sir. Thanks for letting me know." Matthew nodded.

"By the way, whoever did this did an excellent job. I've never seen a better job of TPing."

Matthew smiled in satisfaction as the officer walked away.

CHAPTER SEVEN

Mattie glanced down at the current receipt, thankful that she'd already gone through half of the stack. She checked the amount on the receipt to make certain it corresponded with the statement in front of her.

"I've got some files that need to be returned as soon as you've finished with that," her supervisor informed her.

"Thank you, Cathy. I should be done with this in just a little bit."

"No hurry, but I would like you to get to those today."

"That shouldn't be a problem." Mattie smiled.

She enjoyed this office job, but just wished it paid more than minimum wage. When she asked for more hours, her employer did his best to find some for her. However, when her father called in and told her boss that she wouldn't be coming in, that pretty much forfeited her chances of getting any extra work in the future. Needless to say, her employer was not happy to have to find someone to fill in for her.

At this rate, it would take her forever to get enough money saved up to go to New York. *Wait a minute! Maybe I can borrow some from JJ.* She recalled them saying something about having money saved up for a rainy day. She didn't like to borrow money from other people, but paying it back shouldn't be a problem once she landed a good-paying job in New York.

That's what she would do, she decided. Although she was grounded and not allowed to go anywhere but to work and back, she'd make a quick stop by the Fisher residence to speak briefly with her twin cousins. If anyone could understand her plight, Johnny and Judah surely would.

"Mattie! What do you think you're doing, dressed like that?"

Mattie glanced down at her jeans and sweater, and then stood up straight. This was the moment she'd been dreading – and looking forward to – all day. She took a deep breath and spoke before she lost her nerve.

"I'm leaving, Dad."

"You're *what*?"

"I'm moving out. I'm going to New York."

"No, you're not."

"I'm eighteen now, Dad. You can't keep me here. I'm an adult."

"I forbid you to go. You're not mature enough to make adult decisions."

Mattie shrugged. "Sorry you feel that way. I'm going to do this whether you approve or not. It's my life, and I have a right to live it any way I want to." She couldn't believe she was actually speaking these words to her father.

"What's going on?"

Mattie hadn't even seen her mother walk in the room.

"Our daughter says she's going to New York," her father said.

"Mattie, no!"

"Sorry, Mom, but I have to go. I can't live here anymore."

Tears welled in her mother's eyes and it took all of her resolve not to cry too.

"If you're going to leave against our wishes, that's on your conscience. But don't expect to come back and be part of this family unless you've changed your rebellious attitude and swallowed your worldly pride."

She knew her father meant every word. "Don't worry, Dad. I don't plan on coming back."

Her mother gasped. "Please don't leave, Mattie!"

"Maryanna, let her go. This is what she wants." She heard the resignation in her father's voice. "We can't stop her."

"Bye, Mom. I love you." She leaned over and briefly embraced her mother, and then abruptly stepped out the door. The moment she did, her tears fell freely.

Mattie smiled and turned a complete circle. "Well, what do you think?"

"*Ach*, Mattie! You cut your hair. And your clothes – oh, my goodness! You look so…so different…so *Englisch.*"

"Do you like it?"

"I don't know, but I'm sure some *Englisch* man will."

"I think I'll take that as a compliment." She grinned.

"So, you're *really* leaving."

"Yes, I am."

"Did you tell your folks?"

Mattie frowned and nodded.

"What did they say?"

"My dad forbid me to go."

"Oh, boy. What did you say to him?"

"I just told him that it was my life and this is what I want to do."

"And he let you go?"

"Well, I'm eighteen. He couldn't exactly keep me there."

Her friend's eyes widened.

Mattie chuckled. "Don't worry. It'll be okay." She wasn't sure whether the statement was meant for Elisabeth or herself.

"Are you scared?"

"A little. But I think my excitement overshadows my fears."

"Don't forget about me."

"Are you kidding? You'll probably be receiving a letter from me every day." She laughed.

"*Nee*, you'll be too busy exploring the city."

"I don't know about that. It's going to be pretty expensive to live there. I doubt I'll have extra spending money – at least not until I get a decent-paying job, which I hope will be soon."

"I can't believe you're actually going. I don't know what I'll do here without you." Tears sprang to Elisabeth's eyes.

"Oh, no. Don't make me cry. It'll ruin my makeup." She hugged her friend. "I'm sure you'll be fine. You have Luke Beiler, after all."

Elisabeth sighed.

"What was *that* for?"

"Luke. I don't know…I just…I guess I'm confused."

"You've been courting for a year now."

"I know. I think he wants to get serious about our relationship."

"But you're only seventeen."

"I know. Honestly, I don't think I know what I want yet."

"So, if he asks, tell him that."

Elisabeth frowned. "Maybe I should break up with him."

"Why?"

"Well, I think maybe we're getting too close. Moving too fast…uh, you know."

Mattie's eyes widened. "Lis! You and Luke haven't –"

"*Nee*! I mean, we've kissed a lot and stuff, but…I don't know. I think maybe he wants to."

"Don't you dare!"

"I'm not going to. That's why I'm thinking of breaking up with him."

"If he expects you to do something you shouldn't, you *should* break it off."

"I don't know if that's what he wants or not. He keeps talking about building a house and all that…" She shook her head. "He wants more, but I don't think I can give him the commitment he's looking for."

"Don't settle for something you don't want. You'll live to regret it."

"I know."

"Hey, I'll send you my new phone number when I get settled in New York. Call me anytime you need to, okay?"

Elisabeth nodded.

"Well, I better go before I hit rush-hour traffic."

"Leave a message at the phone shanty as soon as you arrive."

"As soon as I can." A tear formed in her eye. "Don't worry about me. I'll be fine." She pulled her best friend close and hugged her fiercely.

"Bye, Mattie."

"Goodbye, Lis. Hope to see you soon."

Mattie couldn't help the flow of tears as she drove out of the Schrocks' long lane. With each turn of the tires, her best friend faded from view.

Doubts assaulted Mattie and she began to second-guess herself. Could she do this on her own? She didn't know. Whether she could or not, there was no turning back now. Maybe someday she'd return, but she didn't expect that to happen for a long, long time. Paradise, Pennsylvania would now be a part of her history.

She took a cleansing breath and gathered her emotions. This was what she'd been waiting for her entire life! Why was she fearful? Her longtime dream was finally being fulfilled. She could do this. With a burst of excitement,

Mattie rolled down her window and shouted, “Goodbye, Pennsylvania. Hello, New York!”

CHAPTER EIGHT

"Where's Matilda? Why didn't she come along?"

Matthew's blank stare should have communicated the bewilderment he was feeling at his father's direct question. Surely his father had already heard the news. His throat turned dry as he anticipated his father's response. "Mattie's…she's gone."

"Gone?" Sabastian Riehl frowned.

Maryanna quickly filled in, "Mattie left to go live in New York."

Matthew grasped his wife's hand a little tighter, thankful for his helpmeet's presence. She knew relations with his father had always been strained, and she often provided an immeasurable source of comfort. He mentally braced himself for his father's reaction.

"I see." His father nodded. "When will Rebekah be leaving too?"

"Rebekah?" Matthew frowned.

"This is the example you have set for your children, Matthew. One of unfaithfulness."

Matthew's jaw dropped. "Unfaithfulness? I…I don't understand."

"Just as you have not stayed in the place that God set you, your children will not stay. One step in the direction of the world leads to another. Then another. You have begun a cycle that cannot be stopped. I tried to warn you before you–" His eyes went to Maryanna, and Matthew understood exactly what his father was saying. He'd always blamed Matthew's marriage to Maryanna for all the problems that had surfaced over the years.

Matthew grimaced and offered an apologetic glance at his wife. "That has nothing to do with this."

"Doesn't it? Train up a child in the way he should go."

"Mattie was raised in a good Mennonite home. As much as you may disagree, we are not heathens. We have taught our children right from wrong," Matthew asserted.

"If this is true, why did Matilda recently go to jail?"

Matthew sighed. "Mattie is old enough to make her own decisions. Sometimes she makes the wrong decisions, just as we *all* do."

"You have proven my point, Matthew."

Matthew stood up. "I think it's time for us to leave now. Goodbye, Father."

Maryanna had been unusually silent the entire evening since the visit with his folks. Matthew intended to talk to her as soon as the children retired for the evening. Now that supper was over and the house was quiet, the opportunity finally presented itself.

"Want to talk?" Matthew closed the door to their bedroom and turned the lock.

Maryanna shrugged and sat on the bed.

Matthew interpreted her body language to mean that she did want to talk, but she wasn't quite ready yet. He sat behind her and began gently rubbing her shoulders. After a few moments of silence, he stopped and sat beside her.

He took her hand in his. "Was it something my father said?"

Her bottom lip trembled and he knew he'd found his answer. "What if he's right? What if I've ruined your life? What if *I* am the reason Mattie left?"

Matthew shook his head. "Maryanna, you're the best thing that's ever happened to me, after salvation. Don't ever think that you've ruined my life."

"But it's true, Matthew. If you'd stayed Amish–"

"Then I'd be miserable." He reached up and wiped a tear from her cheek. "I chose *you*. I love you, Maryanna. I don't regret leaving the Amish for one minute. I wouldn't want my life any other way."

"But Mattie's gone!"

"That was her choice. We just have to pray that God will watch over her. Maryanna, God loves Mattie even more than we do. I think we can leave her in His hands."

She nodded, and Matthew drew her into his arms and held her close.

"Let's pray and just trust Him, okay?" He pressed his lips to his wife's cheek. "I love you, Maryanna."

CHAPTER NINE

Mattie glanced down at the newspaper in her hand. She crossed off another ad. *Are there any decent apartments that aren't already taken?* Her eyes roamed to the last one on the list. *Where is this?* She punched the address into the GPS and followed the voice commands.

The car rolled to a stop in front of a multi-level, brick apartment complex. She glanced out the window and sighed. *This is not what I had in mind.* Three children, a boy and two girls, maybe six to ten years of age, played a game of jump rope on the sidewalk. Mattie walk past them and they immediately halted their game and stared.

"Wonder what she wants," the boy said to thc girl next to him, most likely his sister.

"Hello. Do you live here?" Mattie smiled.

"What's it to you, lady?" The boy's suspicious stare felt unwelcoming.

"I'm looking for the apartment manager," she said.

"Fred said he already paid the water bill."

"Oh, I'm not here for that. I was looking to rent an apartment."

"*You*, lady?" The boy shook his head.

"Will you tell me which apartment the manager is in?"

"Up the steps, down the hallway, second door on the right." Mattie turned at the sound of a man's voice. He sat on the steps with a small twisted cigarette in his hand; his thick curly black hair that stuck out from his old baseball cap, looked matted.

"Thank you." She hurried up the steps, past the man, and walked into the dimly-lit hallway. Strange sounds emanated from above and brought goose bumps to Mattie's arms. She quickened her step and noticed a door that had an 'office' sign on it. She knocked on the manager's door.

"Enter," a gruff voice from the other side of the door called.

Mattie took a deep breath and stepped into the manager's office. She briefly glanced around and noticed untidy stacks of papers and manila folders on the manager's desk, and on all of the seats but one.

The man cleared his throat. "Yes?"

"I wanted–"

"Look, I just sent off the payment for the water bill yesterday. As soon as these renters pay me, I'll be sending off the electric bill, so please don't cut if off again."

"I'm not here from the electric company or about the water bill."

He rolled his eyes. "Social Services? Not again. I think you know where the Jackson family lives."

"No, I'm not here from Social Services. I was interested in an apartment."

His eyes widened. "Oh, you are?" He rolled his eyes again. "By all means, why didn't you say so?"

Mattie smiled.

"I've got two units available. These aren't the nicest apartments, but we've got great prices. "We require a month's rent in advance along with the security deposit, which is a thousand dollars. So, your total will be four grand."

"Four thousand dollars?"

He took a puff of his cigarette and placed it in an ashtray. "That's right. No pets allowed, and if you're going to smoke, we prefer you do that outside. I'll show you what's available."

Mattie was still reeling from the price when she heard the shriek of a siren.

"Oh, no." The manager continued talking, using words Mattie had never heard before. She guessed that they weren't good words.

"Here are the papers. Just fill them out." He jumped out of his chair and dashed out into the hallway. "This might take a while, miss."

She watched as four police officers rushed through the hallway asking the manager for apartment twelve.

"Third floor. What's going on?" the manager asked.

"We received a domestic violence call." One of the officers placed a hand on his gun holster. "Do you know anything about it?"

"No, sir," the manager responded.

Mattie watched as the officers headed through a doorway. She thought she saw stairs on the other side. The manager hurried after them. She didn't know what they meant by domestic violence, but it didn't sound good.

She glanced down at the papers and shook her head. *I can't live here.*

Mattie left the manager's office and quickly walked back to her car. A bright orange-colored envelope was folded over on her windshield, and she removed it. She looked down at the paper inside and read *The City of New York Notice of Parking Violation.*

"Oh, no."

She looked around and noticed the children were now gone. The man on the stairs had relocated to the steps of another apartment building a few doors down.

Mattie set her GPS to the address of the motel she'd been staying in, and decided to stay there until she could find a decent place to stay, although she had no idea how she would find such a place. All she knew was that her money was dwindling fast. And even if she *wanted* to live at the apartment complex she'd just left, she wouldn't have had enough for the outrageous down payment.

Mattie hurried past the bustling crowd blocking her way. If she didn't get to her interview on time, there would be no chance of securing this job. She'd thought she knew exactly where the building was, but she'd been proven wrong. How was it that, when you're in the midst of them, most skyscrapers look alike?

She paused for a moment, looked up, and glanced around. For an instant, she felt dizzy and quickly closed her eyes. When she felt her equilibrium stabilize, she reopened her eyes. She took a deep breath and told herself not to do that again.

"Excuse me, miss. Are you okay?"

She turned at the male voice and found kind eyes staring back at her. Heat rose in her cheeks. "Um, I, uh, I'm lost," she admitted.

"Where are you trying to get to?"

She studied the young man in the fancy suit for a moment and decided she'd have to trust him. He seemed nice, but one could never know. She lifted the paper she'd written the address on and showed the man.

He nodded and smiled. "You're almost there. It's just on the next block."

"Oh, thank you. I was beginning to think I'd never find it."

"Yes, it would be very easy for one to get lost in this city." He glanced up ahead. "I can walk you there, if you'd like."

"Oh, no, that's not necessary. But thank you."

"No problem." He smiled.

Mattie watched the man disappear into the building they were standing in front of, and briefly wondered if he worked there. When she began walking again, she realized the crowd she'd passed earlier had now passed her by. *Oh well.* She sighed and decided not to pass them again. It wasn't worth the effort.

She tried to walk as quickly as she could. It wouldn't do if she was late for this interview.

"Hey!"

As soon as she turned her head to see what the disturbance was about, she suddenly lost her footing. When she realized what was happening, she attempted to cry out. Searing pain burned her legs as they scraped along the surface of the alleyway. Mattie tried to pull loose from the strong man, who pulled her mercilessly down the frightening darkened corridor.

Her heart beat rapidly. "Please! Let me go," she cried.

"Not a chance," the ruthless perpetrator mumbled.

Her body suddenly dropped to the ground and she winced in pain. It was then she realized the man in the suit had returned and was currently slamming her assailant into a concrete wall. She gasped when the attacker lunged toward the man in the suit at full force and they tussled on the ground beside her.

She momentarily pondered whether she should flee or stay to be sure her rescuer made it out alive. Her instincts told her to do the former, but she didn't have the heart to leave him there alone to fight this monster.

"Run!" the man in the suit commanded.

She briefly hesitated, then did as bidden. Her body ached with each step, but she continued until she reached the sidewalk near the busy street. Mattie looked back, relieved that her attacker fled in the opposite direction. Her rescuer hastened toward her.

"Are you all right, miss?"

She observed his busted lip and the blood that trickled from his hairline. Was he oblivious to his own injuries? Surely he'd sustained more physical damage than she had.

"I think so."

"Your leg looks pretty bad. You really need to get it cleaned up."

She looked down at her leg and discovered a tear in her knee-length skirt; it revealed part of her thigh. She felt heat rising in her cheeks and quickly moved to cover her bare skin.

"I meant your injuries," he chuckled lightly. The man glanced down the street. "My office isn't too far from here. I have some first aid supplies. Come."

Mattie was too weary to argue with him, and, at present, she didn't feel like walking all the way back to her car. She reluctantly nodded.

"Oh, no. My bag!" She looked around frantically. "My papers, my keys, everything's in there."

"Wait here."

She watched the man enter the alley they'd just escaped from. A moment later he returned with her handbag.

"Is this it?"

"Yes, thank you." She looked inside, pleased and amazed all its contents seemed to be accounted for.

"Ready now?"

She smiled and nodded.

A short, but painful, walk led them to a tall skyscraper. Prior to arriving in New York, Mattie had never been inside one. The luxuriousness of their interiors never ceased to amaze her. She wondered how much money it took to build one of these giant workplaces.

"Beautiful fountain, huh?"

Mattie hadn't realized she'd stopped walking, mesmerized by the building's beauty. "Uh, yes. It's very nice."

The man pointed to the elevator. "My office is on the fifteenth floor."

Mattie followed him to a pair of steel doors and waited.

He turned to her. "By the way, my name is Richard Greene."

"Mattie. Mattie Riehl."

"Nice to meet you, Mattie." He held out his hand for her to shake.

Ding. The elevator doors opened in front of them and he gestured for her to step inside. A few moments later, Richard unlocked the door to his office and invited Mattie in.

He gestured to a black leather sofa. "Feel free to take a seat. My secretary's not here today. May I get you something to drink?" He walked over to a small refrigerator.

"Water?"

He nodded. "Sure thing." He removed two bottles of water, handed one to Mattie, and sat on the couch beside her.

"Thank you," – she took a sip – "I needed that."

He smiled. "The restroom is behind that door. You'll find medical supplies and bandages in the cabinet. Use whatever you need."

"Okay."

His brow lowered. "Do you need help?"

"No, I think I can handle it. But thanks for offering." Mattie slipped inside the bathroom, found the hydrogen peroxide, ointment and bandages, and began dressing her wounds. As soon as she poured the hydrogen peroxide over her wounds, they stung, and she let out a subdued cry.

"Are you all right, Mattie?" A gentle knock on the door accompanied the compassionate voice.

"Uh, yeah. It just stings a little." She winced again as she poured more onto her wounds, but took comfort in the fact that it was working, as evidenced by the foaming and bubbling action that removed the debris from her legs.

"You're sure you're okay?"

She chided herself for acting like a baby. "I'll be out in just a little bit. I'm fine."

"All right, then. I'll just take a seat on the couch over here and pretend you're not torturing yourself in there." He chuckled.

Mattie smiled. "You do that."

She didn't know much about Richard, but, so far, he seemed like a nice guy. She briefly wondered if he was single – not that she was looking for a romantic relationship.

After a few more minutes, she emerged from the bathroom. "You wouldn't happen to have any extra skirts lying around, would you?" She held her torn skirt together with one hand, to avoid exposing her thigh.

Richard chuckled. "Sorry, fresh out of skirts."

"A sewing kit?"

He grimaced. "Afraid not."

"Didn't think so."

Richard patted the couch next to where he sat. "Come, tell me about yourself."

"Don't you want to put a bandage on your forehead?" It had stopped bleeding, but it looked terrible.

"Nah, I'm fine."

She realized it was just the two of them in the office, and suddenly felt awkward. "I should probably go now."

"Please don't. I…I'd like to walk you back to your car. Where did you park?"

"At a parking garage a few blocks down."

He nodded. "Are you new to New York?"

"How can you tell?"

"Well, you parked further than necessary. And you didn't know where that address was."

"Yes." She frowned. "I was supposed to go for a job interview there. I don't think I'll be getting the job now. They said they were pretty strict about keeping appointments and punctuality."

"What position were you applying for?"

"Receptionist, but I can do just about any office work." She finally sank down into the sofa.

His lips pressed together. "If I didn't already have a secretary, I'd consider hiring you."

"That's kind of you."

"Where you from?"

"Lancaster County, Pennsylvania."

"Ah, Amish Country. Do you have any Amish relatives?"

"My father was Amish."

His brow rose. "Was?"

"Yeah. He left to marry my mother. They're Mennonite now."

"How about you?"

She shrugged. "I don't know what I am. Nothing, I guess."

"I grew up Catholic, but I'm Baptist now."

"From Catholic to Baptist? That's a pretty big jump."

"Yeah, a funny thing happened when I started reading and understanding my Bible. Just call me Martin."

"Martin? I thought your name was Richard."

He chuckled. "I meant Martin, as in Martin Luther, the Reformer. That's kind of what happened to him. He began reading his Bible and discovered that many things required by the Catholic Church were unbiblical. When he came across the verse that said '*the just shall live by faith*', he struggled with whether he would follow the Catholic Church or follow what he believed to be Truth. If he went against the church's teachings, he risked his very life. However, if he went against his conscience, he'd be risking his soul. I admire him for his courage. It took a lot of guts to do what he did."

"Amish use the Bible he translated."

"That's right. The German Luther Bible, right?"

Mattie nodded.

Richard's fingers steepled in front of his chin. "Mattie, would you be interested in attending church with me?"

"When?"

"This Sunday?"

Mattie grimaced. "I don't know if I'm ready to go back to church yet. I kind of need a break."

He nodded. "Well, when you are, my offer will still stand."

"I appreciate that." Mattie was thankful that Richard didn't argue with her or tell her that she really should go.

Richard glanced up at a clock on the wall. "You have any dinner plans?"

"Actually, I should get back to the motel."

"Motel?"

"Uh, yeah. I haven't found an apartment yet." She grimaced.

"Yikes, I bet that's pricey." He scratched his head and squinted. "Let me see if I can find something for you."

"Really? You'd do that for me?"

He walked to his desk and reached for his cell phone. "No big deal. Besides, I don't know if I'll be able to find something."

Mattie stared at the rip in her skirt and frowned. It was one of her favorite articles of clothing and also one that went well with several different blouses. She'd only purchased two skirts and a pair of jeans, along with a few tops. All of her Mennonite clothing stayed in her closet at home. She figured it wouldn't have been appropriate city attire and quickly discovered she'd been correct.

Richard pressed his phone to end the call and looked to Mattie apologetically. "She doesn't have any rooms available now. I'm sorry."

"Who was that?"

"It was a lady from church who sometimes takes in boarders. She has a few rooms that she rents in a small duplex, but they're all taken right now." He shook his head. "I wish – wait a minute." He picked up his phone once again and dialed a number. "Jackie, would you be willing to rent out one of your rooms?"

While Richard conversed, Mattie wondered who Jackie was.

"Let me ask her." He covered the phone's mouthpiece and looked at Mattie. "Can you do six hundred a month? It's just a room – you'd be sharing a bathroom and the kitchen."

She nodded with a smile. Six hundred a month, even if it was only a room, was a great deal. Most rooms she'd looked into started at twelve hundred and went up from there. "When can I move in?"

"She'll take it, Jackie." He smiled and clicked off the phone. "Tomorrow."

"Who's Jackie?"

"My sister. I know she can use the extra money right now, so I thought she might say yes."

"Does she live alone?"

"She has two kids."

"And no husband?"

"He's in the military overseas. He won't be back for another year."

"That must be hard."

"It is, but she manages."

"My father doesn't approve of the military. He thinks we should turn the other cheek."

"What do you think?"

She shrugged. "I guess I've never really thought much about it. My people have always taught that it was wrong. The Plain people are non-resistant, you know."

"No, I didn't realize that. So, they're pacifists?"

She nodded.

"So, let me get this straight. Your father would have allowed you to be assaulted by that thief if he were with you today? He wouldn't have done anything?" Richard's face darkened.

"I don't know."

"You could have been killed. I don't know how anyone could stand by and watch an innocent person be assaulted. That's ludicrous!"

"They would say it was God's will because He allowed it to happen."

"Since when is sin and hurting the innocent God's will?" He shook his head. "I'm sorry, but I wholeheartedly disagree with their stance. The Bible says that he that provideth not for his own is worse than an infidel. Providing protection for a family that God has entrusted to you is a basic need. I don't understand their position."

"Jesus said to turn the other cheek."

"That's true, but I think that's taking it out of context. That doesn't mean we don't defend our loved ones. *Greater love hath no man than this, that a man lay down his life for his friends.* Soldiers risk their lives every day so we can enjoy the freedoms we do. This nation never would have survived if brave men and women didn't fight for our country."

Mattie was quiet. She really didn't have any response to his words.

"I'm sorry. I tend to get passionate about things I believe in."

"I noticed." She smiled. "Were you a soldier?"

"No. But I'm here if my country ever needs me."

Mattie nodded, then glanced up at the clock. "I should probably go now."

"Was that a 'yes' to dinner?" He smiled.

"I don't know. I'll need to pack my things up if I'm going to move tomorrow."

His brow lifted. "Perhaps, but you still need to eat. Come on, my treat."

She looked down at her clothing and frowned.

"Don't worry. We can stop by the motel first, if you'd like."

"Okay."

CHAPTER TEN

"Jackie, I'd like you to meet Mattie. Mattie, this is my baby sister, Jackie," Richard introduced Mattie to her new landlady.

"Nice to meet you. Thank you for taking me in."

Jackie eyed Richard. "I trust my brother."

"Yeah, usually she'd do a whole background investigation and call references to be sure you'd be a good candidate for renting." Richard smiled.

"You can never be too sure," Jackie added. "There are a lot of unsavory characters out there and I don't want them anywhere near my children."

"I understand. We met one today." Mattie sighed, and gave Richard a smile of appreciation once again.

"Hence, the busted lip and cut above my eye," Richard pointed to his battle scars.

"Who won?" Jackie raised a brow.

Richard chuckled. "That's a tough call."

"I'm just glad we're both still alive and in one piece," Mattie said.

"Me too." Richard winked.

"Miss Riehl, it's good to have you here."

Mattie reached her hand out to shake her new boss' hand. "Thank you for this opportunity, Mr. Bonneville. I will do my best for your company."

He nodded. "Richard Greene spoke highly of you. He recommended that I at least interview you. I'm glad I did."

Mattie's eyes widened. "Richard? You know him?"

Mr. Bonneville smiled. "Richard and I go way back. We're old colleagues. He explained your situation. I'm sorry you didn't receive a positive welcome to New York City. I hope your scuffle in the alley won't taint your view of all New Yorkers."

"I've met several kind folks since I've moved here, so, no, it didn't taint my view. I just learned to be more cautious and to stay far away from alleys."

"Richard says you're from Amish Country."

"Yes, Lancaster County, but I was Mennonite, not Amish."

"I'm not familiar with the Mennonite group. Are they similar to the Amish?"

"Well, there are different groups of Mennonite and different groups of Amish. But the Amish were born from the Mennonites originally."

"So first there were Mennonites?"

"Yes."

"But the Amish seem more popular."

"I think that is because many of them tend to be strict. Most only drive horse and buggy."

"And their dress is…peculiar."

Mattie chuckled. "I think they would like that word to describe their dress. Of course, Conservative Mennonites dress in a plainer fashion as well."

"Is that what you are?"

"Were. And yes, that's the group my family is from."

"How is their dress different from the Amish? Is it easy to tell them apart?"

"It is for me, but it might be a little more difficult for someone who doesn't know the differences. Mennonites tend to wear lighter colors with patterns on them. Amish dresses are usually darker colors with no pattern or design on the material. Of course, like I said, each group pretty much has their own regulations on dress, transportation, how their homes can be decorated… those kinds of things."

"Wow, I think I'd have a difficult time being in one of those religious groups."

"Most people who are Amish were born into an Amish family, so they grow up that way. My best friend is Amish."

"Really? And they allow that?"

"Well, our families are pretty close. The community that I'm from tends to be more accepting, because my grandfather is the Amish bishop there."

"Wait. So your grandfather is Amish?"

"My father used to be Amish and my mother's parents and siblings are still Amish. My mother never has been Amish."

"But your grandparents are? I'm confused."

"Let's just say that it's a *long* story."

"Sounds like it." He rubbed the stubble on his chin. "By the way, there are two things we don't discuss here: religion and politics."

"Why?"

"Let's just say that things go a whole lot smoother when those two subjects are not mentioned."

Mattie shrugged. "Works for me."

"However, what you discuss with other employees after hours is totally up to you."

"Got it."

"Well, it looks like we'd better get to work. I'll have my assistant give you a tour of our office and introduce you to everyone. Every Friday at two, unless you receive a memo stating otherwise, we have a mandatory meeting for all employees." He stretched out his hand. "Once again, welcome to the team, Mattie."

"Thank you, Mr. Bonneville."

CHAPTER ELEVEN

Elisabeth perused the assortment of fabric, searching for the perfect colors for a double wedding ring quilt. Several of her peers were getting married this year, and she wanted to make something special for them. The quilt wouldn't be very large, just a simple lap quilt. Perhaps she should use a different design. *Jah*, she'd make a mini nine patch heart quilt, she decided then and there. She quickly chose some favorite colored fabrics.

"*Hullo*, Elisabeth."

She spun around at the familiar voice. "*Ach*, Rebekah! How are you?" She hadn't seen any of the Riehl family since Mattie had left.

"Okay. I miss Mattie." She frowned.

"*Jah*, me too," Elisabeth sympathized.

"Have ya heard anything from her?"

“Not since she arrived in New York. She left a message at the phone shanty saying she’d made it. Other than that, I don’t know anything.” Elisabeth sighed.

“I hope she’s all right.” Elisabeth heard the concern in Mattie’s sister’s voice.

“I’m sure she’s doing great, Rebekah. If I know Mattie, she’s having the time of her life,” Elisabeth smiled in reassurance.

“I hope so. I just wish I knew for sure.”

“When I hear from her, I’ll let you know, okay?”

“Thanks, Lis.” They quickly bid each other farewell.

Elisabeth watched Rebekah walk out of the store.

“Hey, you ready?”

She turned and looked at Luke, who’d accompanied her today. “Almost. I need to pay for this.”

Luke walked to the register with her and waited patiently while she paid for her items. He relieved her of her bag of fabric and notions and the two of them sauntered out of the store. Luke helped her into his buggy and they quickly set off toward home.

“Beth, where do you see yourself in five years?” Luke’s voice was low.

Elisabeth frowned. “Where did that question come from?”

He shrugged. "Don't know. Just thinkin' about the future is all. Our future."

"Our future?"

He nodded.

"I don't know where I see myself, honestly." She thought of Mattie. "You know, Mattie always knew that she'd go to New York someday. It was a fire that burned deep in her soul. I don't have that fire. I mean, I can't really imagine what my future will be like."

"You don't wish to spend it with me?" She heard the disappointment in his voice.

She shook her head. "I don't know. I'm unsure of what I want. Maybe I'll have a clearer picture in the future, but right now I just can't say."

"I love you, Beth. I really do." Luke swallowed. "I can wait another year, if that's what it takes. I want to marry you someday."

Elisabeth sat quietly. She'd always considered Luke handsome, and he was a kind young man. He certainly deserved to have a good Amish wife. Was she being selfish, keeping him for her beau when she knew she most likely would never marry him? She briefly wondered if maybe she should break up with him.

Luke reached over and grasped her hand.

"I think I might want to taste the *Englisch* life, like Mattie."

Luke frowned. "I was wondering if you were thinking on that. Are you not happy here in Paradise?"

She shrugged.

"We could maybe take a trip to New York and visit Mattie," he suggested.

"*We*?" She frowned. Although she enjoyed spending time with Luke here in Paradise, his joining her and Mattie in New York was *not* a part of the thoughts she'd been entertaining.

"*Jah*, after we're married. I don't suppose your folks would let ya go with me before."

"No, they would never approve of something like that."

"Will you be baptized next year, then?"

Elisabeth cringed. She knew this question would be coming. "Like I said, Luke, I don't know." She was unsure whether he felt the frustration in her tone, but at least it stopped the questions.

"I sold my car," Luke said flatly.

"Why?" As soon as she asked the question, she regretted it. She hoped it wasn't in anticipation of getting married. Usually young folks held on to their vehicles until they were to be baptized into the church and they *had* to get rid of them. Of course, that's why he'd sold it.

He shook his head. "I guess it doesn't matter."

When Luke dropped Elisabeth off, he was unusually silent. She knew she'd disappointed him. He'd wanted an honest answer, didn't he? Well, that was exactly what she'd given him.

"*Denki* for the ride, Luke."

He nodded without comment and set the horse in motion.

CHAPTER TWELVE

Mattie glanced out the window of the high-rise, both thrilling and a little frightening still after three weeks on the job. Even with the other giant skyscrapers surrounding the building she worked in, she still had a decent view of New York Harbor. The view from the twenty-first floor was simply amazing. She didn't think she'd ever get over the grandeur of the Big Apple.

Her heart swelled with gratitude toward Richard for speaking with her boss about her missed interview. She still couldn't get over the fact that Mr. Bonneville and Richard were friends. After Richard informed her boss about the circumstances behind Mattie's missed appointment, he was gracious enough to offer her another interview. She couldn't help but wonder if Richard also put in a good word for her.

Her father had been wrong. There were good people in the city too. Not all the good folks lived in the country. It was true that the people here were more reserved, and most were not as friendly as those in Lancaster County. Although, her home town had its share of snooty people too, she mused.

Richard had been a true friend. She hadn't had too much contact with him since landing her job, but he did check up on her every now and then at his sister's apartment. She got the feeling that he and his sister visited more often now that she was living there. Mattie enjoyed watching Richard interact with his young niece and nephew. The fact that he was good with children hadn't escaped her notice.

Mattie declined his latest invitation to church. Again. For the life her, she just couldn't bring herself to say yes. Of course, her coworkers' opinions of church hadn't help either. She'd have to agree that city folk were less religious than those in her hometown. And it seemed like the ones who were religious believed things she'd never even heard of. She still found it rather odd that discussions of religion were not acceptable or welcomed in the workplace. Wasn't that a First Amendment right or something? She briefly wondered what kind of people attended the large cathedrals with the beautiful stained glass windows she'd noticed while driving in the city. They seemed the exact opposite of the plain, unadorned, simple church house her Mennonite community attended – or of the houses and barns where her Amish friends met for worship.

She thought about her best friend, Elisabeth Schrock. Oh, how she missed her. What was she doing now? Mattie felt guilty that she hadn't even written to her yet. Aside from a brief phone call the day she'd arrived, she hadn't had any contact with anyone in her home community. And, even then, she'd just left a message on the machine for Elisabeth. She'd promised she'd keep in touch, but life seemed so hectic since she arrived. She'd have to make time to pen a letter to her friend, lest she get worried about her wellbeing.

Dear Elisabeth,

You're not going to believe this. I saw you today! Well, it wasn't you but I could have sworn it was. I passed this woman who, if she hadn't been in Englisch clothing, I would have thought it was you. I'm serious! You wouldn't believe it. I heard her say something and even her voice sounded like yours – except for her Englischer accent, of course. She could easily pass for your twin. Hmm...I wonder if I have a twin somewhere out there too! Ha! Ha!

I am so loving New York! You would not believe all the different kinds of people here. It's amazing! Every single day, I see people from probably at least a dozen different countries. Some of them don't even speak English.

The buildings here are so tall. Imagine my grossdawdi's barn about twenty times taller! And that's just the building I work in. Some are much higher than that! It hurts my neck to look up at them from the street.

I'm so glad I took those computer classes in college. If I hadn't, I don't know what kind of job I would have found. If you get a chance, go to the library and use the computers there. I think they have some classes online for free. If you ask one of the library workers, they can show you how to use it. Now, I wish I had shown you while I was there. Just type 'free computer class' into the box at the top of the screen and hopefully it will take you to an online video. You'll need to buy some headphones from the library so be sure to take a few dollars with you. Remember, if you don't know what to do, just ask. They will help you and they probably won't mind doing it. If all else fails, call me and I'll walk you through it. Even if you don't think you'll ever come to live in New York, learn it anyway. You never know how it might come in handy. But I hope you will come! I miss you. Imagine the two of us living together in New York! You'd have a blast, I know it!

How is everyone doing there? Tell Rebekah I miss her, okay? Are Mom and Dad well? How is Dawdi Judah and Mammi Lydia? Other than you, I probably miss them the most. And JJ, of course! Those two got me into so much trouble! I have to admit, though, I enjoyed every minute of it. Except Dad getting on my case, that is. Oh well, I'm just glad I don't have to deal with that anymore!

Well, I hope you'll write me back soon. I'm anxious to hear news from home. By the way, how are you and Luke Beiler doing? Are you still courting? Write me – I need answers! And details. Ha! Ha!

Love ya,

Mattie

P.S. Sorry I haven't written you till now. As you can imagine, I've been busy. And please tell JJ I should be sending them some money in my next letter.

Mattie closed the letter and placed a stamp in the upper right-hand corner. She purposely hadn't mentioned the incident with the thief on the street. If Elisabeth were to *ever* consider coming to New York, Mattie didn't want to give her reasons not to. She'd have enough obstacles in her way already without hearing about the negative aspects of city life. Besides, the good outweighed the bad anyway.

CHAPTER THIRTEEN

Elisabeth's head shot up at the knock on the door. *Rachel*. Her neighbor stood just on the other side of glass – a welcome sight. Elisabeth rushed to the door as soon as her hand towel sufficiently absorbed the dishwater on her hands.

"Rachel." Elisabeth smiled.

Her friend handed over two dozen eggs.

"*Denki*. Our hens just stopped layin' last week. *Daed* said he doesn't know why."

Rachel shrugged. "Ours are still layin' just fine, so I don't think it's the weather."

"Would you like to visit a while?"

"*Jah*, but just a little bit. *Mamm's* got me making pies today."

"That's right. Meeting's at your house this week." They both moved to the table and sat down. "Sweet tea?"

Rachel nodded. "*Denki*."

Elisabeth walked to the counter and pulled a pitcher from the refrigerator. She poured two glasses for herself and her guest and rejoined her friend at the table.

"Have you heard anything from Mattie?" Rachel grinned.

"*Ach, jah.* I got a letter from her last week."

"How is she doing?"

"She sounds great. She loves New York." Elisabeth rubbed the condensation on her glass. "I always knew she would."

"She's not scared over there all by herself? I think I'd be."

"Mattie's always been good at making friends. I doubt she's lonely."

The back door swung open and Elisabeth's brother walked in, his clothes dirty and sweaty from working in the fields. "Lis, will you…" Her brother stopped speaking when he noticed Rachel at the table. "I…uh…" He swallowed.

"Yes, Jacob?" Why on earth was her brother acting so strange?

He shook his head. "Never mind." Jacob turned and walked back through the door he'd entered.

Elisabeth looked across the table at Rachel and shrugged. "I have no idea what that was all about." She laughed.

One corner of Rachel's mouth lifted slightly.

Jacob poked his head in again. "*Dat* would like you to bring us somethin' to drink."

"Can it wait until Rachel leaves? She's not staying long."

"I...I should probably go," Rachel said.

"No. Uh...yeah, that's fine, Elisabeth. We can wait." Her brother furtively glanced at Rachel, then disappeared just as quickly as he'd entered.

Elisabeth shook her head. "My brother's acting *ferhoodled* for some reason."

Rachel stared at her hands.

"What kind of pies are ya makin'?"

"Snitz and peach." Rachel's face brightened.

"You enjoy baking, don't you?"

"Yes, very much so."

"Jacob's favorite pie is peach. I'll be sure to tell him that you're making some."

"I...I could save him one."

"I'm certain sure he'd like that, but you don't have to."

"It's not a big deal, just one extra pie." Rachel shrugged. She drank the last of the tea in her glass. "I'd better go now. I'm sure Jacob and your *vadder* are probably gettin' thirsty, *ain't so*?"

"You're probably right. See ya tomorrow, Rachel."

Elisabeth observed as her neighbor walked back across the field toward her house, then she glanced toward the barn where Jacob was working. Sure enough, he lifted his head and watched as Rachel walked toward her home. When Rachel glanced back, Jacob quickly turned back to what he was doing.

Elisabeth's brow lowered. *Does my brother have a crush on Rachel?* She'd have to ask him about it later.

"Did you get your pie, Jacob?" Elisabeth smiled at her brother as their family enjoyed supper.

Jacob frowned. "What do you mean?"

"Rachel Brenneman said she was gonna make you a peach pie."

He glanced at their folks. "Rachel? What for?"

"I told her peach was your favorite."

"What'd ya say that for?"

"Well, it is, isn't it?"

"*Jah*, but it ain't none of her business."

"But I thought…" She stopped mid-sentence and realized Jacob's attitude was most likely due to discussing this in front of the family. "Never mind. But she did make a pie for you."

"I don't want no pie from Rachel."

"Jacob Schrock, that is an ungrateful attitude to have." His father eyed him from across the table.

"I don't want no girl making me pie."

"Well, you didn't mind her riding with ya," his younger sister commented.

Their father's brow rose.

"Hush, Martha. That ain't none of your business," Jacob grumbled.

"But I saw you and Rachel on your horse," she insisted.

"Martha, that's enough. What Jacob does is his business," their father warned.

"I don't know why he don't want the pie." Martha shook her head. "I'll take it. I love peach pie too."

"You're not gettin' my pie," Jacob said.

Martha frowned. "But you said–"

"That's enough, *kinner*." At their father's warning, the conversation at the table died down.

Elisabeth couldn't help but wonder about Jacob and Rachel, though.

Jacob sighed as he approached the Brennemans' back door. *Mamm* insisted that he pick up the pie that Rachel had made for him. He would have much rather stayed home and sent Lis to get the pie.

The door opened just as he was positioned to knock. “Jacob?”

He dropped his hand and it suddenly became clammy. Just looking at Rachel Brenneman always did that to him. “I…uh…” If only the lump in his throat would appear at a different time. “Pie.”

Rachel frowned. “Would you like to come in?”

He shook his head. “Come inside? No.”

“You wanted pie?” Her brow lowered.

“Peach pie.”

Rachel laughed, then her eyes sparkled in recognition. “Oh! The peach pie I made for you. I’ll get it. Come in.”

Jacob did as bidden, but stayed just inside the door.

“*Jah*, Lis told me that ya liked peach pie. I told her it wouldn’t be a big deal to make an extra one for ya.” She moved to the cook stove where a pie sat atop the warming rack.

“*Denki*.” It was all he could manage.

Saul, Rachel’s father, entered the kitchen. “Jacob?”

He didn’t miss the look that passed between Rachel and her father, although he couldn’t decipher its meaning.

“He’s just here to pick up his pie, *Dat*,” Rachel informed her father.

“I thought you gave the last one to John Hostettler,” her father said.

Jacob's gut tightened. *John Hostettler?* He'd seen him eyeing Rachel at the last singing but didn't think twice about it. Perhaps he should've been a little more vigilant.

"*Nee*. Not the last one," Rachel replied.

Saul nodded in satisfaction and continued out the back door.

"Would ya like me to put it in a box for ya?" Rachel asked as she held the pie.

"Uh, no. This is fine." Jacob's mouth began watering at just the thought of taking a bite. It had been many months since his last peach pie. If he wasn't in Rachel's presence, he'd probably take a bite or two now. It certainly wouldn't remain untouched until he returned home.

"Here ya go."

Her cheerful countenance made him remember all the reasons he liked her. She was sweet and spunky, and would surely make a good wife for some blessed man someday. "Uh, Rachel, would you like to come see the new filly that our mare birthed last week? We could maybe go for a ride too."

Rachel's cheeks tinged pink and Jacob thought her beautiful. "I, uh, I can't."

Did she have plans with John Hostettler? "Oh." He frowned. "Fine. I just thought I'd ask. I thought that maybe…uh, I–I better go."

"Okay. Goodbye, Jacob."

He nodded briefly then stepped out the door. If she was interested in John, why had she gone riding with *him*? She shouldn't have led him on if John was courting her. Perhaps she was one of those girls who'd court several boys before finally settling down with one. Well, if that was what she was doing, he certainly wouldn't be the one who was played for a fool. Even if he considered Rachel Brenneman the prettiest girl in Paradise, he refused to lay his heart open for her to trample on.

He glanced down at the peach pie in his hands. It probably wouldn't taste as good as he expected, given his mood. He slid his fingers between the pie plate and the crust and lifted a slice to his lips. He was wrong. It was every bit as delicious as he'd imagined. If only Rachel Brenneman only had eyes for him…

It would be a match made in Heaven, for sure and for certain.

CHAPTER FOURTEEN

Mattie finally finished unpacking the remainder of her things. She glanced down at the black book in the back of her car's trunk – a Bible. No doubt her father had something to do with its presence. She shook her head and slammed the trunk closed.

"No thanks, Dad."

She sighed and hurried back up to her room in the apartment she shared with Richard's sister. She'd been lucky to find a decent place for a great price. She'd have to remember to thank Richard again.

Mattie smiled, thinking of her date tonight. She'd finally agreed to let Richard take her out, after making excuses the several times he'd asked. He was certainly a persistent man, which spoke volumes to Mattie. If he wanted to get to know her that badly, he must see something in her worth pursuing.

She briefly pondered the possibility that he could be the one. Was she ready for a serious relationship? She purposely hadn't made any serious romantic ties back home because she knew that someday she'd leave. But, now that she was here, what was stopping her from pursuing romance?

Richard seemed to be pretty much everything she'd ever wanted in a man. He'd been gallant in every aspect of the word – opening doors for her, tending to her wishes, allowing her the first of everything. He seemed truly selfless, and his chivalry in rescuing her from the thief in the alley hadn't escaped her notice either. What kind of man was willing to risk bodily harm for a complete stranger? And, while he wasn't a cover model for any popular men's magazines, he was handsome in his own right.

Just one thing made her hesitate. His regular church attendance. She'd been dragged along to church her entire life, and by no means did she wish to continue down that road. Now that she was finally free from all that bondage, she couldn't imagine stepping back into it willingly.

"I've got a surprise for you." Richard's mysterious smile piqued Mattie's curiosity.

"What is it?" She waited as Richard punched in the number to the lobby.

Richard shook his head. "Nope. If I told you, it wouldn't be a surprise now, would it?"

Mattie smiled and gathered her bearings while the elevator came to a stop. It was always that last part that made her stomach flutter. The elevator doors opened and they walked into the lobby.

"My lady." Richard offered his elbow to escort her and she placed her hands in its crook. They walked to the door and Mattie looked around.

"Where's your car?"

He pointed to a white limousine parked by the curb. A man in a fancy suit stood by the back door of the vehicle. Richard walked forward and the chauffeur opened the door. "Ladies first."

Mattie's jaw dropped and she stared at Richard.

"Well, go ahead. We don't want to miss our engagement." Richard motioned to the car.

Mattie climbed into the limousine and sat on one of the cushioned seats. Richard slid in beside her.

Mattie looked at Richard in wonder. "This is the first time I've ever seen the inside of one of these. It's so fancy."

"What do you think?" Richard smiled.

"Oh, it's wonderful! Did it cost a lot of money?"

Richard's grin broadened. "You're not supposed to ask questions like that."

"I'm not?"

He brought her hand to his lips. "No. Just enjoy it."

"Are you going to tell me where we're going?"

"Nope. You'll just have to wait and see."

"I feel like a princess!" She giggled.

"Mattie, you are a princess. And I aim to be your Prince Charming." His eyes sparkled.

"You're doing a great job." She moved closer to him.

"I hope so."

Mattie set her fork down and savored the last bite of her baked halibut. She determined this was definitely the best meal she'd ever eaten. Everything on her plate had been absolutely delicious.

How is it that Richard intuitively knew exactly what she'd dreamt of for the last two years of her life? The dinner theatre had been everything that she'd hoped it would be and more. She was certain that no day of her life would ever compare with this evening. She was living her dream!

Tomorrow, she'd write Elisabeth and tell her all about it. The only thing that could make her world better is if her best friend were here, sharing in all these wonderful experiences.

Richard had been a perfect gentleman. When he said goodbye for the evening, he kissed her cheek and handed her a single red rose. He didn't ask to come inside. He didn't ask for anything, in fact. It seemed his sole existence for the evening was to indulge Mattie's every whim. Anything she wanted, he provided. If only every night could be this wonderful. Yep, Richard knew how to treat lady – he was a true Romeo.

CHAPTER FIFTEEN

The cool breeze in Mattie's face felt invigorating. Richard squeezed her hand a little tighter as the two of them walked through Central Park together. This was officially their second date. Compared to the last one, it was simplistic, but Mattie cherished her time with Richard just the same.

"Tell me more about you," Richard coaxed.

"Be more specific." She smiled.

"Okay. Let's start with your views on God. What do you believe?"

"You had to start with an easy question," she teased.

Richard chuckled. "You said be specific."

"I know. May I retract that request?"

Richard shook his head. "Too late."

"You don't play fair." Mattie laughed. "Okay. Well, I've pretty much gone to a Conservative Mennonite church my whole life. We dressed how we would say 'modestly', meaning the women would wear dresses that went to at least mid-calf, but preferably to the ankle. Our sleeves usually would be at least to our elbow or longer. Our necklines would come to about our collarbone. All our dresses were handmade."

Richard nodded. "Interesting, but not exactly what I was asking about. I want to know what *you* believe right *now*."

"Oh. Well, I guess I believe in God. Doesn't everybody?"

"No, everybody does not. What do you believe about Jesus?"

"That He's God's Son."

Richard blew out a breath. "What does that mean to you?"

Mattie's brow lowered. "What do you mean?"

"Does He have any significance in your life?"

"Well, we celebrate His birth at Christmas."

"Why?"

She shrugged. "I guess I've never really thought about it."

"Seriously?"

"Well, in school we would have a Christmas program. My church taught that Jesus was the Saviour of the world. But, honestly, for myself, I'm not into religion."

"What do you mean by that?"

"Has anyone ever told you that you ask a lot of questions?"

"Yes, all the time. Why?"

"See what I mean?"

Richard chuckled. "Seriously, though. What do you mean when you say you're not *into* religion?"

"I'm just not interested in all that."

"Why not?"

"There you go again. Well, I guess I just feel like it's been forced on me my whole life. You know what I mean?"

"I think so."

"Can we change the subject?"

"Sure. What would you like to talk about?"

"Anything but religion."

"Politics?"

"Or politics."

Richard laughed. "Good. I don't particularly care to talk about politics either. So, did you grow up on a farm?"

"Yep. Don't miss it. You?"

"I've never lived on a farm. We always lived in town. I've heard farms are stinky."

"Well, farms typically have animals. Animals don't usually make use of the sewer system." She held her nose for emphasis.

"I hear you. I can see why you don't miss it." He laughed. "How do you like New York so far?"

"Oh, I love it!"

"You don't miss your family?"

She shrugged. "Some, I guess. But I'd have to say I miss Lis the most."

"Your sister?"

"No. My best friend. I'm hoping that she'll come here one of these days. I keep telling her how awesome it is."

"Do you think she'll come?"

"I don't know. It'll be even harder for her. She's Amish."

"You don't see too many horses and buggies in New York City."

"Only fancy carriages once in a while. Yeah, it would be difficult for her, for sure."

"Well, I'm glad you came." Richard smiled down at her and brought her hand to his lips.

"Yes, so am I." Mattie smiled.

Greetings, Mattie!

New York sounds like such fun! I hope I can come visit someday. Luke said we can take a trip there after we get hitched, but I was hoping to go sooner than that. Besides, I'm not sure what I want to do just yet.

Things are going fine here. Everything is pretty much the same. I think Jacob might be thinkin' of courtin' Rachel Brenneman. I'm pretty certain sure they like each other. I think they'd make a good match, ain't so? Well, I guess only Gott knows that.

Your fancy Englischer sounds real nice. I'm glad you found a good man.

I miss you, Mattie. I miss our talks, even though yours were always about New York. I'm glad you're *happy. I feel lonely here without you. It would be wonderful gut if we could see each other again!*

Your gut friend,

Lis

P.S. JJ said thanks for paying them back the money.

CHAPTER SIXTEEN

Matthew stared at the calendar on the dining room wall. He flipped through the previous months and admired the photographs on each page. A large red circle caught his eye and he sighed. It had been six months now since Mattie left.

Lord, was I too hard on her?

He never thought any of his children would desire something different than the life of blessings God had provided for them. *God, You said to train up a child in the way he should go and when he is old he will not depart from it. I'm trusting that verse. I don't know what Mattie's doing, Lord. Is she ruining her life? Please send someone to minister to her. Please keep my precious daughter safe and let her return to You.*

Matthew wiped a lone tear. He'd never been one to cry before Mattie left, but it seemed his resolve had broken down. A father's heart could only bear so much. *How did You do it, Lord? They even mistreated Your Son. How could You handle that?* That was something he was sure he'd never understand. But man wasn't meant to understand God's ways. *Lord, help me to trust and obey.*

He turned the calendar back to the current month and walked into the kitchen. His wife turned from the stove and must've noticed his contemplative countenance.

"What's wrong?" Maryanna frowned.

"Just thinkin' about our daughter. You know, she's been gone for almost six months now."

Maryanna nodded silently.

"I'm just wonderin' if she'll *ever* come back home." He hated the fact that he couldn't stop the tears from pricking his eyes.

"Why don't you write her a letter?"

"She hasn't sent her address to us. I have no idea where she even is."

"She's in New York. I can't imagine that she hasn't contacted Elisabeth. I'm certain she'll have Mattie's address."

"I'm not much for writing. I don't know. What would I write?"

Maryanna took his hands in hers and gazed into his eyes, the way she had so many times over the last twenty years. "I'm sure God will give you the words to say."

He nodded and swallowed hard. Although they'd had their share of arguments over the years, when he was feeling down, Maryanna always knew what to say to him. "All right."

Mattie didn't bother to check her mailbox every day because she seldom received mail, and when she did, it was usually junk mail or bills that had come due. It had been nearly a week since she'd last checked the box, and Jackie had been out of town. So, with key in hand, she sauntered to the hallway where the boxes for the renters were located.

She sifted through the mail, removing Jackie's things, but throwing most of it away. The last item caught her eye. *Paradise, Pennsylvania?* The handwriting look somewhat familiar, but it certainly didn't belong to Elisabeth. She'd wait until she was back in the comfort of her room to devour the letter from whoever.

Mattie sat on her favorite comfy chair, a Papasan chair is what Jackie had said it was called. She stared at the letter and attempted to decipher the handwriting. It didn't belong to Lis or Mom; as a matter of fact, it didn't look like it was written by a female. JJ wouldn't have written to her, would they? For the life of her, she couldn't figure it out.

She finally opened the letter and immediately read the last word. Dad. Mattie stared at the letter for nearly ten minutes before reading it. She was tempted to tear it up and throw it into the trash can, but then she'd never know what its contents held.

She took a deep breath.

Daughter,

I'm not one for writing letters. I don't really know what to say except that I miss you.

Mattie stopped reading. *Really, Dad? Somehow I can't believe that.* She shook her head and continued reading to see what other ludicrous statements her father had to make.

I know we haven't always gotten along. Wasn't that the understatement of the year? Mattie rolled her eyes, but continued. I admit some of that was my fault. I didn't always know how to handle you. I apologize for my lack of knowledge in that area. If I've said hurtful words to you, please forgive me.

I hope you are happy in New York. I hope you have found whatever it is you've been searching for.

Mattie, please don't abandon God. I've been praying for you and will continue.

Dad

Richard's index fingers steepled in front of his chin as he peered at Mattie. "So, will you write your father back?"

Mattie shook her head. "I don't have anything to say to him."

"I don't think that's true." Richard frowned.

"When I left, my father told me not to come back. Just because he's feeling bad about my leaving doesn't mean I do. I'm happy in New York."

"Even so, shouldn't you at least acknowledge that you received his letter?"

"Why should I, Richard?"

"Honor? Respect?"

"I've lost all my respect for my father. I won't write him back."

"I think you should."

“Yeah, I know. Can we please change the subject?”

“If that’s what you’d like.”

“Yes, it is. So, where are we going for dinner tonight?”

“Chinese?” His brow shot up.

“Sounds good to me. Then what?”

Richard leaned close and nuzzled her neck. “We can go back to my place.” He studied her expression, waiting for her protest.

“That sounds nice.”

He leaned back and frowned. “Really?”

She shrugged. “If you want to.”

“Mattie, don’t tempt me like that.”

“You suggested it.”

“Well, yeah, but I didn’t expect you to say yes.”

“What if I am saying yes?”

“Don’t. *Please*. Because I don’t know if *I’m* strong enough to say no.”

Mattie laughed. “Did I find your weak spot, Richard?” she teased.

“Yes, that would definitely be my weak spot.” He shook his head in an attempt to clear it. “It’s getting hot in here. We’d better go.”

CHAPTER SEVENTEEN

Elisabeth smiled at Luke, splashed water in his direction, and then quickly bobbed under the water's surface to dodge his vehement retaliation. Fortunately, she was several feet away from him and not within reach.

"You know there're consequences for bad behavior," Luke teased.

"You gotta catch me first!" She pushed more water in his direction.

At his charge, Elisabeth swam as fast as she could to the edge of the pond. She ran along the shore, with Luke in hot pursuit. When he lunged at her, she jumped back into the water and swam for dear life. A firm grasp on her ankle told her she'd been caught.

"Oh, no you don't!" Luke laughed.

"*Ach*, let me go!" She giggled, but feigned offense and wriggled wildly.

"Not until you give me what I want first," he insisted.

"What's that?"

"A kiss."

"Then you'll let me go?"

His gaze smoldered. "I don't intend to *ever* let you go, Elisabeth Schrock."

She understood his hidden meaning. Out of breath from struggling to get away, she finally conceded. "Okay, I give up."

"Really?" Luke pulled her close.

Elisabeth nodded.

The moment Luke's lips met hers and he chuckled, she knew she'd fallen into a trap. When Luke lifted his hands from her neck and shoulders, cool mud remained in their place.

"Luke Beiler, I'm gonna get you for that!" she threatened.

"Oh, I hope so!"

She quickly reached to the bottom of the pond, grasped a handful of mud, and charged after him. Luke leapt from the water and ran toward their picnic blanket.

"No fair!" Elisabeth stopped to catch her breath. "I can't keep up with you."

"It's about time you realized that." He smiled. "Drop your weapons and I'll stop."

"Fine."

He looked back to be sure she released the mud from her hands.

She held up her hands. "See? No mud. Are you happy now?"

He sauntered toward her. "Uh-huh. I'm always happy when I'm with you."

"Stop right there!" She thrust her palm out toward him. "Let me see *your* hands."

"Why?"

"Because I don't trust you. How do I know you're not armed?"

He lifted up empty hands. "There. Now, are *you* happy?"

She nodded.

"Good." He ran toward her full force.

"Luke, what are you doing?" Elisabeth laughed.

Her question was answered swiftly when he lifted her from the ground and spun her around. She'd never seen him so joyful. "What if I asked you to marry me?"

He set her back down so she could gather her bearings.

"Luke…"

His gaze turned sober. "It's been almost two years."

"I know." She frowned.

"How long do we have to wait, Beth?"

She shrugged.

"Please don't say no." Elisabeth didn't miss the emotion in his voice.

"Then don't ask. I'm not ready."

His fists clenched momentarily. "I love you, Elisabeth Schrock."

"I know."

Luke frowned. "Please don't make me wait forever."

She stared into his mesmerizing blue eyes and lifted a half smile. "I won't."

Hi Mattie,

How I wish you were here to talk to! I miss you. It's not the same with you gone. I'm so tempted to come see you.

I feel torn. Luke is a good beau, really he is. He's been hinting at marriage and I'm really not comfortable with it. I really don't think it's him; it's me. I've been discontent here lately. Things that never really bothered me before bug me now. My folks seem to be on my case about everything lately, so I can totally relate to how you felt with your dad. How is that going, by the way?

I look at the Englisch world and there's something about it that sounds so appealing. What is it like to wear whatever you feel like instead of what your folks and church leaders say you can wear? What's it like to have a phone in your purse and be able to call someone at any time? I have so many questions for you.

Remember what you said about those computer classes? Well, I've been learning some. I like it a lot. I think I would enjoy a job like that. It's a lot more fun than I thought it would be. It would sure beat milking cows every morning and churning butter.

Well, I should go now. If you think about it, please pray for me. I need to know what to do. By the way, Richard sounds really nice!

Sincerely,

Lis

CHAPTER EIGHTEEN

Richard stopped in at his sister's apartment after church to see Mattie. It was a ritual he'd begun when they'd started dating. He'd hoped that eventually he'd be able to persuade Mattie to join him, but so far his efforts had been fruitless. Honestly, he felt like giving up sometimes.

"Mattie, will you *ever* come with me to church?" He hoped he didn't sound as desperate as he'd been feeling lately.

"I don't need church."

"Everyone needs church."

"Why? People can worship God anywhere."

"I agree with that statement partly. We can worship God anywhere and everywhere, but that doesn't mean that people don't need church. God is the One who ordained the church. He set it up. He knew that we would need a place to find love and encouragement and fellowship with other believers. For

Christians, it gets tough in this world. We need all the support we can get. It's a lifeline of sorts."

"I have everything I need without all that."

"Well, for someone who's been saved, I can tell you what it's like to be without a church family. It's like a coal that has been removed from the fire. Without the other coals to help produce heat and warmth, that coal will go out. With the help of the other hot coals, that single coal will eventually light on fire."

"Church never really meant all that much to me."

"I'm sorry to hear that." Richard shook his head. "I've got a revelation for you, Mattie. Church and everything else in this life is not about *you*."

"Did I ever say it was?"

"You didn't have to."

"That was rude."

"I'm speaking the truth in love."

"Is that what you call it?"

"Mattie, how can I get you to see? Here's the problem. When we take our eyes off Jesus and only focus on ourselves and our circumstances, we can no longer see Him. God says that He will keep us in perfect peace if we keep our eyes on Him."

"Is that in the Bible?"

Richard didn't miss the sarcasm in her voice, but he would use her question as an opportunity to show her what the Bible had to say. After all, God said that His Word would not return void. And right now, Richard would take any and every opportunity he got, no matter how small.

"Yes," he quickly opened the black book in his lap before she could protest, "Isaiah, twenty-six, verse three says *Thou wilt keep him in perfect peace, whose mind is stayed on thee, because he trusteth in thee.* Anytime I feel my peace slipping, I know it's because I've taken my eyes, and, thus, my mind, off Jesus. Where is *your* focus, Mattie?"

"Well, apparently I don't need God. I have all the peace I need."

"Do you really?"

"Yes."

"Why did you come to New York, Mattie?"

She swallowed. "Why?"

Was she stalling for time? "Yes, why?"

"Well, I – I wanted to."

"Is that the only reason?"

"Yeah, why?"

He'd hoped she'd answer honestly so he didn't have to call her out on the carpet, but it seemed he had no choice. "It didn't have *anything* to do with your family? Your *father*?"

"Wh–" She frowned. "Why would you think that?"

"Be honest, Mattie."

"The only–" Her eyes moved to her desk. "Wait a minute. Have you been reading my mail?"

"Answer my question first." He folded his arms firmly across his chest.

"Maybe. Yes, my father is partly why I left when I did."

"Have you forgiven him?"

"I already answered your question. Answer mine now. Did you read my mail, Richard?"

He nodded once.

"I can't believe it! You really did read my mail? My letters are *personal*. You had no right to do that!" Tears pricked her eyes.

"Would you have told me the truth otherwise?"

"Maybe there are some things that I'd rather not have you know about, Richard. Did you ever think of that?"

"Mattie, when two people love each other, they don't keep secrets." He rubbed her arm.

She stepped away. "Oh, yeah? Well, when two people love each other, they don't sneak around behind each other's backs and read their private letters either!"

"Mattie…" Richard sighed. "I only did it because I care about you. I care about us. I'm sorry."

She shook her head. "That's not good enough, Richard."

"What else do you want me say?"

She shrugged.

"Well, I should probably go then." He walked up behind her and gently placed a kiss on her cheek. "Goodbye, Mattie." Richard ambled to the door with a heavy heart. There were so many things he wanted to say but they'd have to wait. If he and Mattie were to have any future together, they would definitely need to work through their differences. Had he been a fool in hoping that Mattie could change?

CHAPTER NINETEEN

"Would you like something to drink?" Richard offered.

"White Zin?" she said, half teasing, just to get a reaction out of him.

He frowned. "You know I don't do alcohol. How about a sparkling water?"

"Strawberry?"

He handed her a plastic bottle and smiled.

Mattie stared at the artwork on the wall in Richard's office. It seemed they hung out there quite a bit after hours because it provided privacy and quietness from the bustling outside.

"Will you ever consider becoming a Christian?"

Leave it to Richard to ask the difficult questions. Why is it that every conversation lately seemed to end up in a discussion of religion?

"Who says that what you believe is right? There are hundreds of denominations and religions out there. What makes you think the way *you* believe is right?"

"I admit that everything I believe might not be right. I'm fallible. I don't claim to have all the answers. Total trust in God does require a small amount of faith. I do, however, think that God makes it pretty easy to believe. There is proof of His existence everywhere. I just look up at the sky at night and stand in awe. Or, how about the ocean? Isn't it amazing how it just stays in its place and doesn't flood the rest of the world? That's something that the Bible talks about. Just look at the abundance and diversity of plant life and the way all of life sustains itself. I think a person would have to try awfully hard to convince himself that God doesn't exist.

"You know, Mattie. What you believe or what I believe doesn't really matter. When life is all said and done, the only thing that will matter is the Truth. We have a choice to believe it or not. God won't ever force it on anyone.

"I do wonder, though, Mattie. What would it take for *you* to believe?"

"Please, Richard."

"Are you not even going to consider it?"

"I told you already that I'm done with religion."

"Well, if that's what you want."

"It is."

He nodded and stood up from the sofa. His Adam's apple moved as he swallowed. "I guess this is goodbye, then."

"Goodbye? What do you mean?"

"I'd thought that maybe you were the woman that God had planned for me. I was wrong."

"So, that's it? You're just going to end our relationship because I disagree with you?"

"No, Mattie. It's much more than that. God is everything to me. I'd hoped that I could convince you to put your trust in Him. That's why I've been holding out on asking you to marry me. And, even though I truly love you, I can't risk marrying an unbeliever. It would spell misery for both of us, and I think you know it."

Marry? Mattie's jaw dropped.

"You have a key to my office. Let yourself out when you're ready, and give the key to Jackie tonight, please." Richard leaned over and kissed her forehead. "Goodbye, Mattie."

He walked slowly to the door and hesitated, as though he would say something else. Instead, his shoulders slumped and he left.

As though in a trance, Mattie watched Richard walk out the door. She didn't speak a word. She didn't get up from the couch. She simply stared at the now-closed door. There was nothing to do now. She'd blown it.

The only man she'd ever loved was gone.

CHAPTER TWENTY

Mattie heard the phone ring in the living room. She never answered the phone because she knew Jackie would answer it. Besides, the only person who'd ever called for her on that phone was Richard, and that was when he couldn't get a hold of her on her cell phone. But she knew *that* wouldn't be happening any time soon. The phone rang again and she heard Jackie holler something about giving the kids a bath.

Mattie rushed into the living room and quickly picked up the receiver. "Hello."

"May I speak with Jackie Windsor, please?" a professional-sounding woman on the other line asked.

"Jackie's not available right now. May I take a message?"

"Yes. Please inform her that Richard Greene has been admitted to St. Luke's Hospital. Have her call as soon as possible, please."

"Richard? What's wrong with him? Why is he in the hospital?"

"Who's asking?"

"My name is Mattie. I'm a friend of the family."

"I'm sorry, ma'am, but I'm not permitted to divulge personal patient information over the phone. I'll need to speak with an immediate family member." The lady proceeded to give Mattie the phone number to the hospital and urged Jackie to call as soon as possible.

As soon as she'd hung up the receiver, Jackie walked into the room, followed by two freshly bathed children, as evidenced by their wet hair.

"Who was that?"

"That was the hos–" Mattie glanced at the children. "Uh, St. Luke's. Richard's there."

Jackie frowned. "Children, go dry your hair now."

The children's faces demonstrated their protest, but they promptly obeyed anyhow.

As soon as the children disappeared from the room, Jackie turned back to Mattie. "What's wrong with Richard?"

"I don't know. The lady wouldn't tell me anything. She left a number for you to call." Mattie handed Jackie the paper she'd written on.

Jackie was already dialing the number before she'd taken the note from Mattie's hand. "I'm calling about my brother, Richard Greene. He's a patient there." Jackie waited in silence for nearly thirty seconds. "Yes, Richard Greene. I'm Jackie Windsor, his sister."

Mattie swallowed, anxious to hear the outcome.

"He did? When? Is he okay?" Jackie frowned. "Unconscious." She glanced at Mattie. "Okay. Thank you." She quickly scribbled down a number.

"What happened?"

"They're not sure. Richard collapsed in his home. Fortunately, he wasn't home alone. If he had been, he wouldn't have gotten treatment." Jackie bit her nail. "I need to go see him. Would you mind watching the kids for me? They should go to bed soon, anyway."

"Sure." Mattie watched as Jackie quickly gathered her purse and explained to the children that Mattie would be watching them.

Jackie whispered to Mattie, "I'll call you as soon as I know anything."

Mattie nodded. "Thanks. I'll try to wait patiently."

"And Mattie," Jackie's countenance turned sober, "it wouldn't hurt to say a prayer for him."

"I will," she promised.

Mattie grabbed the phone the second she felt the vibration. "Jackie? How's Richard? What's going on?"

"Mattie, take a deep breath and calm down."

"Okay, okay, I'm calm. Please, how's Richard doing?" She clenched her fist, not realizing her nails were digging into her skin.

"It's his heart, Mattie. The doctors say the condition is something he was born with."

"Will he be all right?"

"They think so. They want to keep him here for a couple of days so they can run tests. I okayed it. He's still unconscious."

"May I come see him?"

"As soon as I get home. How are the kids doing?"

"They're fine. They're asleep."

"Would you mind staying here with Richard overnight?"

"No, of course, not."

"All right. I'll let the hospital staff know you're coming. I should be home in a bit."

"Okay, thanks for calling me."

CHAPTER TWENTY-ONE

Mattie frowned when she walked into Richard's hospital room.

"Oh, you must be Mattie."

She stared blankly at the scantily-clad woman who held Richard's hand.

The woman rose from the chair at Richard's bedside. "I'll be leaving now. Do have Richard call me when he can."

Mattie awoke from her stupefied slumber. "And you are?"

"I was with Richard when he collapsed. I'm Amber. Amber Sexton."

Figures. "Okay, I'll tell him," she lied.

When the woman bent over to kiss Richard's cheek, Mattie was thankful he was still unconscious.

Mattie sighed in relief after Amber left the room. She moved to Richard's hospital bed and sat in the chair beside him. Richard's strong body seemed so weak, lying helpless in this place. She watched his chest rise and fall, and she quickly closed her eyes to prevent a tear from cascading down her cheek.

What if Richard had drawn his last breath? What if his heart did indeed stop its beating? Now that she'd met Richard, she couldn't imagine a life without him. She didn't *want* to imagine a life without him. He was the best man she'd ever met.

God, please don't take him. Please let him live. Let him be okay. He needs You. I need You. And I need him.

It wasn't much of a prayer, but it was sincere.

Mattie reached down and took Richard's hand. It had been too long since these hands had caressed her face, since she'd felt his strong arms around her. She wasn't certain of too many things in life, but she knew that a life without Richard would be a lonely one.

"Mattie?"

She was in a field of wildflowers, wearing a flowing white cotton dress. Richard stood off in the distance, his arms stretched toward her, holding a bouquet of the wildflowers that surrounded them. He was handsome, as usual, wearing a charcoal grey suit. His eyes glimmered and Mattie felt love within their depths.

Mattie attempted to walk toward him, but something invisible blocked her way. Richard called out to her, beckoning her to come to him. But no matter how passionately she tried, she failed to make progress. If she could only break free from this invisible force that held her back. If she could only make it to the safety of Richard's arms.

"Mattie."

She awakened with a start. "Richard?" She looked around to find she was in a hospital room. Mattie suddenly remembered the circumstances surrounding her presence there.

Richard grinned.

"Richard, you're awake!" Mattie smiled in relief and engulfed Richard in an embrace.

"And so are you." He lightly brushed the hair from her face with his fingers.

"I was dreaming. But I couldn't figure out if it was a dream or a nightmare."

"Was I in it?" He smiled.

"Yes."

"Then it was probably a nightmare," he teased.

Mattie shook her head. "How are you feeling?"

"Okay, I think. What happened?"

"You collapsed. They said it had something to do with a heart condition?" Her brow lowered. "What heart condition?"

He shrugged. "It was something I was born with, I guess. I have an enlarged heart."

"What does that mean?"

"For some people, it means very little. They go through life and it doesn't affect them. For others, well, let's just say they could experience an early death."

Mattie frowned. "Maybe that was the invisible wall I couldn't get through."

"What?"

"My dream. You were calling to me, but I couldn't get to you no matter how hard I tried. It was as though something, some invisible force, was holding me back."

"Mattie, I think that was God calling to you, not me."

"No, it was you."

"There is only one thing keeping you and me apart. It's the devil. He doesn't want you to have life and peace and love. He comes to kill, steal, and destroy. I chose Jesus. I chose life. You must choose who you will serve. We all must choose."

"Can we talk about this later?"

"When? Mattie, I might not have a 'later'. If I do die early, I'd like to know that I'll see you again someday."

Tears welled in Mattie's eyes. "Richard, don't talk that way."

"This is reality, Mattie. Not everyone lives forever in a fairy tale world, at least, not on this side of eternity."

"I don't want to live without you, Richard."

"You can live without me, but you can't live without God. Mattie, I'm nothing without Jesus in my heart. You wouldn't even like me if you knew how I was before God stepped in and cleaned up the mess I'd made of my life. The man you see now would not exist without Him."

"What are you saying?"

"I'm saying that God can do things in your life that you've never dreamed of. He doesn't want to drag you down. He wants to lift you up and mold you into who He created you to be. He wants to give you a light so bright that it reaches the whole world and extinguishes the darkness. He can do the impossible in your life if you allow Him.

"Mattie, God will be there for you when no one else is. He will walk with you on every mountain. He will carry you through every valley. He will never leave you or forsake you. You don't need *me*; you need *Him*. I cannot be all those things for you. Only God can."

"I just don't know about all this – this religious stuff."

"It's not about religion at all. It's about having a relationship with our Creator. Mattie, when you heard I was in the hospital, did you pray for me?"

"Yes."

"Why?"

"I felt so helpless. I didn't know what else to do. You were beyond my power."

"That's exactly right. We have nothing, we are nothing, without God. Mattie, God loves you more than I ever could. He wants you to know Him. He wants you to trust Him."

"I'm scared."

Richard grasped both of her hands and searched the depths of her eyes. "I know you are. And so does God. But you don't have to be scared, Mattie. Nothing surprises God. He sees every bend and bump in the road."

"Will you pray with me, Richard?"

"I feared you'd never ask."

"I don't know what to say."

"Tell God what's on your heart. Ask Him to be your Saviour. He's the only one who can fulfill all your needs. Mattie, do you believe in Jesus?"

"Yes. He came to earth as God's Son, and He died and was resurrected to give us everlasting life."

"That's right. Eternal life is available for everyone, but only those who receive Him as their Saviour will become children of God. Mattie, if you want to receive Jesus, all you have to do is ask."

Mattie nodded, bowed her head, and poured out her soul to the only One who had the power to change her life.

CHAPTER TWENTY-TWO

Mattie quickly shoveled cereal into her mouth to prevent her stomach from rumbling during church. If Richard was on time, he would be arriving in about ten minutes. She took a sip of her coffee then looked up at Jackie.

"Who was that woman in Richard's hospital room?" She frowned.

Jackie lifted a half-smile. "Amber? She's one of Richard's old flames."

"I didn't think he'd be interested in someone like that."

"I hadn't seen her since before Richard got saved. I don't know why he was with her." She eyed Mattie curiously. "Why does it matter to you? I thought you and Richard were through."

"Yeah, but…never mind. It just doesn't make sense to me."

"What doesn't?"

"Well, Richard left because I wasn't interested in his religion."

"I think you mean because you weren't interested in God. There's a big difference."

Mattie shrugged. "Whatever. Do you think what's-her-face is interested in God?"

"Probably not."

"Well, then why–"

"Mattie, you'll have to ask Richard. Frankly, what he does is none of my business. If you want to know about Richard's life, ask him."

Indeed, she would ask.

Richard pushed the doorbell and heard its result through the apartment door. A small thrill danced in his belly at the thought of Mattie finally joining him for church this morning. How many times had he prayed for this day?

"Richard!" Mattie's smile warmed his soul.

"You ready?"

"Uh, yeah. Let me just get my purse." She disappeared momentarily.

Richard stepped into the apartment. "Hey, sis. Don't wait up for Mattie. I plan on keeping her for as long as possible."

Jackie's knowing smile told him she was glad to see him happy and healthy. "You know, Ryan will be coming home next month." Her countenance lit up at the mention of her husband.

"I bet you and the kids are ready for that."

"*We* are."

Richard nodded in understanding. Mattie would need to find another place to stay. "I'll find something."

Mattie emerged from the bedroom. "Sorry, I needed to brush my teeth."

"Not a problem. Let's go?" Richard offered his elbow.

Mattie seemed unusually quiet as they drove to church.

"Penny for your thoughts."

She looked at Richard. "I've been thinking about something. Or someone, rather."

"Oh, do I know this someone?"

She frowned. "Yes."

His quizzical look must've given him away.

"The woman at the hospital – the one who was with you when you collapsed."

He nodded. "Ah…Amber."

"Amber Sexton. Is that her *real* name?"

He shrugged. "Don't know. Guess I never thought to ask."

"Who is she?"

Richard loosened his collar. Was it getting hot in there? "Uh, I'm not sure you want the answer to that question."

"If I didn't want it, I wouldn't have asked."

"She's a former, uh…"

"Lover?"

"I didn't want to use that word."

"But that would be the correct one, right?"

He nodded once.

"And you're dating her *now*?"

Richard's brow shot up. "Now? No, of course, not," the words shot out faster than the car that had just passed them.

"I don't understand."

"Truthfully, this is what happened. Amber called me up and asked what I was doing. She asked if I wanted to meet with her and I agreed. Any door that God opens for me to share His love with someone who doesn't know Him, I walk through it."

"I don't know how I feel about that." She stared out the window.

Richard sighed. "Mattie, if you're looking for a perfect guy, I'm not him. The guy *you* met was the guy with Jesus in His heart. But I haven't always had Jesus. I have a past – a pretty dark one, honestly. Before I got saved, I was a child of the devil. I behaved like a child of the devil. If you want someone who has been pure his whole life, I can assure you that it is *not* me. I'm sorry if I've disappointed you."

"I just thought…"

"That I've always been a good guy? I'm flattered, but it's not true."

"But you never said anything about it before."

"Honestly, I'd like to leave the past where it belongs – in the past. My former life is not something I'm proud of. I thank God every day for saving me out of that life. He's been good." Richard reached for her hand. "Mattie, I know I don't deserve someone like you. You're special."

Mattie sat quietly for the remainder of the drive to church, and Richard was dying to know what she was thinking. He really wished she'd say *something*. Had he blown his chances with her by telling her about his past? Was this the end of their budding relationship?

God, if this is the end of Mattie and me, please give me the grace to get through it.

CHAPTER TWENTY-THREE

"Okay, so you said you had bad news for me?" Mattie tasted the metal in her mouth, a common occurrence when grinding her teeth.

Richard peered at her over his open menu. "You want to discuss this now?"

"Why not?"

"I guess there's no time like the present." He set his menu on the table next to his drink. "Ryan's coming home."

"Jackie's husband?"

He nodded. "You'll need to find another place really soon."

"Wait a minute. If this is a proposal, I'm totally not ready for it."

"Proposal?" His flummoxed expression told her it was anything but that.

"Never mind."

Richard chuckled.

"I just made a fool out of myself, didn't I? That was embarrassing." She felt her cheeks darkening. "Can we just rewind and delete that thoughtless statement I just made?"

"That's what I love about you, Mattie; you just speak what's on your mind."

"You do?"

"Very much so."

"Even if I just made a fool out of myself?"

"I thought it was kind of cute actually – you proposing to me," he teased.

She tossed her cloth napkin in his face. "I did not!"

Richard laughed. "Seriously, though, about your living situation…"

"I hate apartment-hunting."

"I know how you feel. The last time I typed in 'cheap apartments in New York City', I think my computer laughed at me."

Mattie smiled.

"I do have some good news." Richard nodded to the waitress, and they placed their order.

"You do?"

"Remember the lady that I told you about at church?"

"The one who rents out rooms in her duplex?"

"Yes, that's the one. She just informed me at church *today* that she and her husband purchased a small apartment complex. They're looking for responsible renters."

"How much?"

"That, I'm not sure of. But I know it won't be terribly expensive. If you could find someone else who would share the cost of rent with you, I think you'd be able to afford it quite easily."

"I know there are always young college students looking for places to rent, but I don't know how responsible they'd be at keeping up with payments."

"Pray about it and see if God won't open up a door for you."

Mattie smiled. "I think I'll do that."

Mattie glanced up from her meal and saw a familiar young man walking toward their table. Where had she seen him before?

"Richard?" The man thrust out his hand.

Richard quickly wiped his mouth with his napkin and greeted the man. "Carson. Hey, great to see you."

"You, too."

Richard grinned broadly. "Mattie, have you met Carson? He just started attending church a couple of months ago."

"No, I don't think so. Nice to meet you," she said.

"Richard led me to the Lord a few weeks ago." The man beamed. "Let me tell you, Richard. It's been a little rough, just like you said. But I'm hanging in there."

"Your friends giving you a hard time?" Richard's knowing look said he'd been through a similar situation.

"My girlfriend, actually." He frowned.

"I'd be willing to speak with her, if you'd like," Richard offered.

"Oh, no, she's definitely not ready for that. She won't even give *me* the time of day regarding the Lord."

"I know exactly how you feel." Richard nodded in understanding. "I'll pray for her."

"I really appreciate that, man. I need all the help I can get."

"Carson, would you like a little advice?" Richard asked.

"Sure. Shoot."

"Sometimes what we want doesn't always line up with what God has planned for us. He might have something better in mind than you have for yourself."

"I hear you." He nodded.

Richard looked at Mattie. "And then sometimes God surprises us and does give us what we want."

Carson looked from Richard to Mattie. "I'm sorry, I forgot your name."

"I'm Mattie." She locked eyes with Richard across table and smiled. "Richard's girlfriend."

"It was good meeting you. I'd better let you two finish your meal."

"Goodbye, Carson." Richard waved as Carson walked away.

Mattie felt his eyes on her, but she pretended to ignore him.

"Girlfriend? Does this mean–" Richard's gaze turned sober.

"Yes, Richard. That's exactly what it means."

Mattie smiled as Richard bowed his head and, no doubt, whispered a brief prayer of thanksgiving.

CHAPTER TWENTY-FOUR

Dear Mattie,

I've made my decision. I'm coming! Please pray that I don't lose my nerve. If all goes well, I'll be leaving Sunday night after everyone has gone to bed. I'm so excited! And scared. I'll see you at your apartment soon, if God wills.

Lis

THE END

A sneak peek at

Amish by Accident

J.E.B. Spredemann

Prologue

Elisabeth Schrock yawned as Minister Fisher's voice droned on and on about how he deemed it necessary for their Amish youth to flee from the things of the world. *You've got to be kidding, right? His boys are some of the most unruly in our district. He must be preaching to his own* kinner. It took everything she had to not snicker and roll her eyes. Of course, his twins were in *Rumspringa* just as she was. *I've heard all this before. It's always the same old thing. The world is wicked; we must live by the rules of the Ordnung…blah, blah, blah.* Her discontentment and restlessncss had been growing daily, along with her rebellious attitude. She was sure that if she had to sit through this for another Sunday, she would burst.

She reached inside her hidden apron pocket and clutched

the letter she'd received from her best friend, Mattie Riehl. Mattie left her conservative Mennonite community a year earlier and now worked in a fancy skyscraper in New York City. She said she'd met a wonderful *Englisch* beau and is happier now than she'd ever been. Mattie encouraged Elisabeth to come visit and even offered to share her apartment if she decided to stay long-term. Oh, how she longed for freedom! She was aching to escape the monotony and endless rules and restrictions of the church. *I'm going to do it!* She decided resolutely.

A cough drew her attention to the men's side of the room. She glanced up to see her handsome beau, Luke Beiler, looking at her curiously. He must've sensed her musing and raised his eyebrows in question. *How am I going to leave Luke? He's ready to join the church and be baptized, but I just can't do it right now. There's too much out there that I haven't seen or experienced. I know that if I agree to be baptized this fall with Luke, he'll ask me to marry him.* Elisabeth hung her head. Indeed, leaving would be the most difficult decision of her life. Nevertheless, she was determined to do it. Today.

Leaving his hot coffee, Luke stood up from the breakfast

table when Jacob Schrock beckoned him to the porch outside. It was indeed strange for Elisabeth's brother to be visiting on a Monday morning, with all the chores he had to tend to and what not. But Jacob's sober countenance gave pause for concern. His friend held out an envelope to him. It was Beth's handwriting. *For Luke.* He searched Jacob's face for a sign as to what the contents might be, but Jacob kept his gaze on the wooden boards beneath his feet. Without a word, Luke opened the letter that would forever change his life.

Luke,

I'm sorry. I just don't feel like I belong here with the Plain people in Paradise anymore. Whether I will come back or not, I do not know. Please do not try to find me.

Elisabeth

Heartbroken. It was the only word that could describe Luke Beiler as he let Elisabeth's letter slip through his fingers onto the hard wooden floor. All his hopes and dreams for the future, dashed into a million pieces with just a smidgen of ink on plain white paper.

Enjoy coloring? Check out various adult coloring books available from Blessed Publishing, including our Amish-themed title.

Thanks for reading!

To find out more about J.E.B. Spredemann, join our email list, or purchase other books, please visit us at www.jebspredemann.com. Our books are available in Paperback, eBook, and Audiobook formats.

A SPECIAL THANK YOU

I'd like to take this time to thank everyone that had any involvement in this book and its production, including my Proofreaders, my Editor, my CIA Facebook friends who have been a tremendous help, my wonderful Readers, my longsuffering Family, my awesome Street Team who, I'm confident, will 'Sprede the Word' about *Englisch on Purpose*! And last, but certainly not least, I'd like to thank my Precious LORD and SAVIOUR JESUS CHRIST, for without Him, none of this would have been possible!

Made in the USA
Columbia, SC
07 September 2020

19624323R10126